THE TIME OF
THE YOUNG SOLDIERS

THE TIME OF THE YOUNG SOLDIERS

by Hans Peter Richter

Translated by Anthea Bell

KESTREL BOOKS

KESTREL BOOKS
Published by Penguin Books Ltd
Harmondsworth, Middlesex, England

Originally published 1967 by Verlag Alsatia, Paris

First published Great Britain 1976
Second impression 1978

ISBN 0 7226 5122 8

Printed in Great Britain by
Lowe & Brydone Printers Limited, Thetford, Norfolk

S02834

St. Columba's High School,
Dunfermline.

Contents

A young nation arises, ready for war!
Comrades, raise your banners higher!
We feel our time is coming,
The time of the young soldiers.
Ahead of us, with tattered, war-torn banners,
March the dead heroes of the young nation.
Above us, our heroic fathers gone before!
Oh Germany, oh Fatherland, we come!

(Words and melody: Werner Altendorf)

Dulce bellum inexpertis.
(War is pleasing to those who do not know it.)

                  (*Erasmus of Rotterdam, 1469–1536*)

If children would only stay children, you could go on
telling them fairy tales for ever.
But since they grow up, the fairy tales must stop.

                  (*Bertolt Brecht, 1898–1956*)

When the war broke out, I was fourteen years old; when it ended I was twenty. I was a soldier for three years. I thought that the things I saw and the things I did were justified because no one spoke out openly against them.

Hans Peter Richter

At Home

'I just can't get on with these ration cards,' my grandmother grumbled. She poured out malt-coffee for us all from her big metal coffee pot, and slid a piece of fruit pie on to my plate.

'Come now, it's not going to be for long.' Grandfather was trying to cheer her up. 'More likely than not we'll get by with what we have stored in the cellar, and you won't need the coupons at all!'

And then the sirens began to wail.

We knew that sound, from all the air-raid practices we'd had – but now it was war. This was a genuine air-raid warning!

There sat Grandmother, petrified, staring at us in terror. Then, with a sudden futile movement, she swept together everything she could lay hands on. The china plates and cups clattered, and coffee slopped over the oilcloth on the table.

Jumping up, Grandfather scurried into the living-room, where he got the tin box containing his papers out of a cupboard and took it down to the cellar. When he came back he tried to calm Grandmother's fears. 'It's only a practice,' he kept assuring her. He repeated something he had read in the paper: 'It will be impossible for any enemy aircraft to invade the skies of the Greater German Reich!'

Once Grandmother had recovered from the worst of her fright, however, she still sat at the table as if she were paralysed. The table itself looked like a bombed site.

Taking my hand, Grandfather led me out of the kitchen. We went through the scullery and out into the garden, where we stationed ourselves by the trunk of the big pear tree, staring up at the sky through its leafy roof.

There were men in other near-by gardens too. One of them had his gas mask in its container slung around his neck; another was scanning the sky with a pair of binoculars.

It was a peaceful day; all was quiet, there was not a sound to disturb the silence, and even the birds were not singing. The sun shone down from a clear blue, cloudless sky.

A neighbour called something out, and pointed. Then we too heard the faint hum. I was first to spot the plane. It was so high you could hardly make it out as it flew on its way, unmolested.

'Just a scout,' stated Grandfather, dismissing it with a wave of his hand. 'They'll soon get tired of that sort of thing!'

The double door opened without a sound. It was a very large room, almost empty. Light fell through the tall windows on to a dark, solid desk.

A man rose from behind the desk. He seemed to be grey all over: his hair, his glasses, his suit, his tie, everything about him looked grey. His footsteps made no noise as he came towards me, inviting me in.

The door closed behind me.

We shook hands, and he offered me a leather armchair. 'Well, so what brings you here?' he inquired as we sat down.

'I'm looking for a job,' I said.

The man bowed slightly from the waist. 'And you've picked this firm? Well, that's nice to know. Thanks for the compliment.' He leaned back in his chair. 'We can do with more people on the job,' he told me. 'In fact, we can hardly manage these days; the war means more work for us, but then it takes my best men for soldiers. Do you mind if I ask your age?'

'I'm fourteen,' I said.

'Have you brought any references?'

I got some papers out of my pocket and handed them over. 'Excuse me,' he said, before glancing through them. After a moment or so he said, 'You haven't left school yet, then?'

'No, I'm still at school,' I said. 'I just thought I might get a job here during the holidays.'

'Are the schools still on holiday?' he asked, in some surprise.

'Well, you see, war was declared during the holidays,' I explained. 'So they were extended. Indefinitely.'

He sounded disappointed. 'That's a pity . . . I thought you wanted to be apprenticed to us. But like this we don't know how long we could count on you. When are these holidays supposed to end, eh?'

'Oh, not till the end of the war!' I confidently assured him.

The man's roar of laughter echoed right through the big room.

We met on the corner as usual, in a covered porch where we could shelter from the rain. Four or five of us, the eldest being nearly twenty years old, would meet there nearly every evening; we all lived in the area. And we talked about the war.

One boy gave us a whole list of those of his relations who had now joined up. 'Just about everyone except for my old man; they haven't taken *him* yet,' he said, evidently not too pleased. 'I tell you, I can't stand it much longer; we have rows every single day. I'd volunteer myself if I was old enough.'

'I *have* volunteered!' said the eldest of us.

'Huh, they won't take *you*!' someone else told him. 'Remember when you tried volunteering for the Labour Service? They wouldn't have you there either!'

The other lad dismissed all objections with an airy wave of the hand. 'Ah, but it's different now. They really need men this time! I'm strong and healthy – what d'you bet they take me this time? Even me!' He rubbed his hands. 'You wait! You'll be seeing me in field-grey pretty soon now!'

'Oh, and what's in it for you?' inquired the sceptic. 'Do you want to leave your mother to fend for herself?'

The older boy shook his head. 'That'll be all right! They'd never touch a soldier's mother. Believe you me, the moment I'm in uniform they'll let my mother alone. I'm going to join the Army, and everything will be all right!'

'What's all this about his mother?' I whispered to one of my neighbours.

He whispered back. 'He's half Jewish, you see.'

The phone rang at about three in the morning. The Red Cross nursing sister, still dazed with sleep, lifted the receiver and listened. She said simply, 'Yes,' and hung up again. Wearily, she turned to us. 'Get the coffee ready – there's a transport on its way.'

We jumped up from our camp-beds at once, lit the gas, and waited till the coffee in the big pans was bubbling. Then we ladled it into cans and carried the hot, black brew down to the platform.

The train was not in yet, but a solitary woman stood underneath a dimmed light, picking nervously at the string round a small parcel she was carrying.

On duty with us at the station were some girls from the B.D.M. (the *Bund Deutscher Mädel*, or League of German Girls). As they waited, they tried to rub some colour into their cheeks, which were still pale with sleep, fixed their hair and smoothed down their blouses. They were ready to meet the train with a smile when it came in.

There were only a few soldiers looking out of the windows; they seemed to be exhausted, and hardly said a word. We poured the coffee, and the Red Cross sister handed out cigarettes.

Meanwhile, the woman with the parcel was walking down the platform, along the line of carriages. 'Josef Schenker!' she kept calling. 'Josef Schenker!'

No one replied to her.

The soldiers at the carriage windows shrugged their shoulders, or else glanced back into their compartments, repeating the name, and then shook their heads. The station-master appeared on the platform, wearing his red cap.

Seeing him, the woman began to run, crying, 'Josef! Josef!' in panic. She waved the parcel as she ran.

The station-master was still waiting. We stood on the station steps with our cans watching the woman search.

'Josef! Josef!'

The station-master shrugged his shoulders sympathetically, and gave the signal for the train to leave.

The woman stood by the last carriage, crying out desperately, 'Josef,' tears streaming down her face. Slowly, the train began to move off.

'Josef!' She was running along beside the last carriage, the distance between herself and the train increasing rapidly. 'Josef!'

Suddenly a window was pushed down in a carriage somewhere in the middle of the train. A soldier leaned right out, waving both arms. 'Mother!'

The train left the station and disappeared into the night, leaving the weeping mother behind on the platform, still clutching her parcel.

I paced up and down the kitchen with the newspaper in my

hand. 'Once again the German infantry have covered themselves with glory. The marches they have made, the hardships they have endured, are no less impressive than their victories in battle. Their courage in attacking was complemented by an indestructible tenacity which enabled them to rise triumphant over the worst of odds . . .' I folded the paper and put it behind my back. I began repeating the passage I had been reading under my breath . . . 'Once again the German infantry . . .'

My mother was sitting at her sewing machine by the window, taking a tuck in the sleeves of a shirt, to shorten them. She turned round, irritated. 'Don't keep marching up and down like that, you're disturbing me! If I don't watch this carefully I shall break the needle.'

I sat down at the kitchen table and buried myself in the paper . . . 'Thanks to the superb leadership, the intensive training and modern weapons of the German Wehrmacht, its successes have entailed casualties on our side which, compared with the enormous losses suffered by the enemy, must be considered remarkably few . . .'

'Oh, stop whispering!' Mother snapped. 'It's driving me crazy!'

I read the final paragraph in silence . . . 'Yet again, the German people can regard its Army with pride, while the Army itself looks forward to further tasks ahead in the confidence of victory.' I put the paper down, closed my eyes, and tried to repeat the whole piece over to myself from the beginning.

My mother looked at me in annoyance. 'How long have you been learning that thing off by heart?'

'Since twelve o'clock.'

'Aren't you ever going to get it finished?'

'Well, it's almost a whole page of the newspaper,' I pointed out.

'A whole page?' said Mother, surprised.

'It's a piece about the Wehrmacht, and I'm learning it off by heart so I can recite it at the victory celebrations at school!'

We were on our way home from the rifle range with our guns slung from our shoulders, raising a lot of dust, because we were dragging our feet. The way back to town led through fields and meadows.

Suddenly the warden who had been instructing us in the use of the weapons stopped. 'Over there!' He pointed left. 'A hundred metres off. That bush on its own.' He raised one thumb and squinted past it. 'Over to the right of it – a thumb's breadth over to the right – enemy marksman!'

There was a tabby cat sitting in the meadow. She did not move.

'Target detected!' we chorused obediently.

'We'll take him by surprise!' said our instructor. 'At the word "three", open fire.'

We unslung our rifles, took cartridges from our ammunition cases, loaded, and raised our guns to the firing position, each of us resting his weapon on the shoulder of the man just ahead.

'One!' the instructor counted.

We took aim at the cat.

'Two!'

We drew back our triggers, as we had been taught.

'Three!'

Our shots rang out almost simultaneously.

We did not do too badly. With a fearsome shriek, the cat leaped about a metre into the air, and then tore away.

'Done it!' said the instructor, satisfied. 'Enemy in retreat!'

'Well, we should get a bit of sleep in peace tonight, for a change,' said Mother. 'No air raids or air-raid shelters here!'

17

We put out the light, pulled back the blackout curtain and opened the window. Then we climbed into the high farmhouse beds, taking deep breaths of fresh air, and lay making plans for our holiday until we fell asleep.

I was the first to be woken by the humming sound. Soon afterwards, a siren, worked by hand, went off down at the village school. We heard a lot of activity going on around the farm; someone ran out to the stables, and the farmer climbed up to the barn loft.

'They're not used to this kind of thing!' Mother chuckled. 'Why would anyone drop bombs here? Let's stay put.'

I went back to sleep again.

At dawn there was a hammering on our bedroom door. Before I was properly awake, I heard Mother ask, 'What is it?'

'Get up!' cried the farmer's wife.

'But it's only half past four!' said Mother.

'The Farmers' Leader wants us.'

'Whatever for, so early in the morning?' asked Mother.

'Everyone has to go,' the farmer's wife told her.

'And this is supposed to be the first day of our holidays!' I grumbled as I got out of bed.

All the villagers were assembled at the farm owned by the man who held the official post of Farmers' Leader for the district. So were the holiday visitors. Most people were carrying buckets about a quarter full of water.

The local Farmers' Leader divided us up into groups, assigning each group to a different area of the village. Since we were strangers here, he included us in his own group. We all set off across the fields, fanning out as we went.

Soon the Farmers' Leader bent down for the first time to pick up a small, square, flat object, about the size of the palm of his hand. He pointed to a yellow spot in the middle.

'Impregnated with phosphorus.' he told us. 'As soon as the sunlight gets to them, these things ignite. *They* –' and he jerked his chin skyward – 'they hope to destroy our harvest with them.'

That first day I found twelve such incendiary devices, though my mother got only three. Some people came back with their buckets half full.

We had real meat broth, potatoes and peas and a thick slice off the joint, and even chocolate pudding, because we were visitors.

After dinner, while the others had a rest, I went out to the farm buildings to look at the animals. It was there, in the barn, under the steps leading up to the loft, that I found the cubicle which had been partitioned off.

The prisoner of war was in this cubicle, squatting on a camp bed without any bedding. When he saw me he nodded. He was eating strong-smelling cabbage soup from a bowl held between his knees. He smiled at me, and asked, in halting German, 'You 'ave *vacances*?'

'Holidays,' I translated, coming closer.

He repeated, ' 'Olidays.' Then he added, 'I not speak German good,' and smiled again. 'Where you come from?'

I described our home to him while he ate. When he had finished, he put the bowl down and produced a drawstring bag from under his bed. He loosened the string and took out a little bundle of photographs, holding out the top photograph to show me. 'My wife, my children, my 'ouse.' Then he pointed to his two sons, and to me. 'Per'aps – friends!' He shrugged, regretfully.

I nodded. I didn't know quite what to say, so I admired the picture of his house.

He seemed pleased. 'I am architect,' he explained. Then he

showed me pictures of other houses, of schools, of office blocks, even a small church. 'I built!' he said proudly, and turned the photographs over. Each place was named on the back of the pictures, and had the date when it was built written underneath the name. The prisoner of war began hunting for some more photos.

Suddenly the door of the building was pushed open, and the farmer looked in. 'You, Frenchy! Get a move on!' he shouted. 'There's that mucking-out to do yet!'

The bomb had fallen in the garden, squashing the little house like a cardboard box. All who had escaped from the ruins, as well as many of the neighbours, had been working through the night. In the morning we too were called to come and help.

My aunt was the only person standing idle by the heap of ruins, crying. People told us she had not stopped crying for over three hours.

My uncle worked tirelessly, clearing away the rubble, hauling stone after stone away from the cellar entrance until the way was clear. His face was dusty, his hands were bleeding, but he paused in his work only to drink.

While the old folk salvaged those household utensils that could still be used, the men shored up the remains of the gable wall, and the rest of us cleared the road with shovels, stacking the bricks that could be re-used by the roadside.

When my uncle came up from the cellar carrying a board, my aunt cried, 'Over to the right a bit more! I'd stood the bottled cherries on that!' My uncle got some helpers and climbed down again.

I slipped down after them, but all I could see in the darkness of the cellar was a heap of rubble as tall as a man below the ruined gable wall.

'In here,' my uncle told the other men.

Bits of stone and mortar were piled in the other corner of the cellar. It took them half an hour to dig my cousin out.

I would not have recognized him.

The men stood around the disfigured corpse in silence, folding their hands. One took off his dirty hat and scratched his head; then, bending down, he picked up a twisted piece of metal.

'His plane,' said my uncle, quite calmly. 'The plane he wanted.' His voice began to tremble. 'We gave it to him for his tenth birthday, two weeks ago.' Suddenly he collapsed on the heap of rubble beside my cousin and wept out loud, as if he would never stop.

The bus came to a halt when we reached a small village. 'We've arrived!' said the driver. 'Everyone out!' His German sounded odd, as if he spoke it with difficulty.

The teacher jumped out first, stationing himself by the door to help out anyone who was exhausted. We had been travelling by special train for two whole days and nights (the train had been running several hours late), and had then gone the rest of the way by bus.

Worn out, the little boys stumbled out and assembled on the footpath branching off from the road, while the driver unloaded the luggage and stacked it up by the roadside. He showed the teacher which way to go, and then drove off again.

The boys had to pick up their own cases and boxes. Very slowly, we climbed the hill, stopping frequently to rest. The path got narrower and even steeper, eventually becoming a mere track. Finally it brought us to the top of the hill, and the hostel.

The warden of the hostel met us at the door; he had

everything ready, with tables laid and hot soup. But the boys were too tired to eat. All they wanted was to fall into bed, though the afternoon sun was still shining. The warden helped us to allot the boys their dormitories, and then invited us to join him in the common-room. After I had washed, I went down, along with the teacher.

The teacher went over to the big window of the common-room and looked out. There were hills and woods in the sunlight as far as the eye could see.

'Well, the lads will soon be feeling better here,' said the teacher. 'A bit of peace from air raids, a proper night's rest – do 'em the world of good!'

Some birds flew up outside the window.

'Lovely!' he said, enthusiastically; he made an expansive gesture. 'And all of it German land, won back for us again! Beautiful!' he repeated. Then he began making plans. 'We'll get to know the villagers! Do our best to bring these people a bit of German culture! They've had to do without it too long. We'll have social evenings with them!' His voice was rising. 'Put on amateur theatricals for the locals! Train their boys and girls to . . .'

'I shouldn't think you'd have much luck,' said the warden of the hostel, coming up. 'Most of them don't speak anything but Polish.'

The master wrote a formula on the board, and then turned to explain it. He walked up and down the rows of desks as he talked. Suddenly he stopped, quite close to me.

The boy in front of me was reading a war book, holding it under the desk so that no one could see it from the front of the class. He never even noticed the master standing beside him. 'Hey, look at this!' he whispered to his next-door neighbour. 'There's a bit here where . . .' Only then did he notice the other boy's rigid attitude, and the general silence. Sitting up straight, he saw the master, and quickly hid the book he had just been showing his neighbour under the desk.

'I see you think it unnecessary to follow the lesson!' said the master, quietly enough. 'You'd rather read, would you? Just what one might have expected, judging by the standard of your work!'

The boy addressed slowly got to his feet, hands resting on the desk top, but he said nothing.

'Does it ever occur to you that you get your leaving certificate in just three months' time?'

The boy was looking out of the window.

'And you needn't expect anything very laudatory from me!' said the master, getting more heated. 'I shall be rating you on your marks – and they're hardly good enough to get you a very creditable certificate!'

Unimpressed, the boy was now cleaning dust out of the penholder groove with his forefinger.

'This school has no place in it for someone like you!' cried the master. Breathing heavily, he turned and marched out of the classroom.

The culprit watched him go, yawned, dropped into his seat again, brought out his book from under the desk and went on reading.

'Why do you needle him like that?' someone in the middle row asked. 'He really *will* muck up your leaving certificate if you keep on.'

The boy in front of me put his book down on the desk. 'Why would I need a leaving certificate at all?' he said. 'I volunteered to join up ages ago!'

They had been coming in ever since the first light of dawn: singly and in whole families. Their faces were still smeared with soot or covered with brick dust, the men's hands were shaking and the women were crying. They carried cases or rucksacks containing their last few possessions, and they looked helplessly around.

We led them to the cold marble-topped tables, brought their things in after them, brushed down their coats and asked what they would like. The girls took charge of babies and toddlers, or listened patiently as hysterical men and women talked to them – talked and talked, of falling bombs, ruined houses, burning buildings.

Meanwhile the Red Cross nurses handed round plates of soup or mugs of hot coffee. A man was going round the tables with a long list, asking for details of the night's casualties and writing down the names of those who were still missing, buried in the ruins, or burnt to death.

Those who had escaped went over the names of the people who had been in the air-raid shelters with them, counting on their fingers, and usually getting it wrong. If they remembered someone else later, someone who might still be among the ruins, they called back the man with the list, and he added that name to it.

The door of the house, which used to be an inn, was opened. We boys were called out. There was a car outside loaded up with banners. While the man went round completing his list of casualties, we nailed the first banner up above the bar. It bore the words: 'We will never surrender!'

One of the Red Cross sisters beckoned us into the kitchen, where she gave us some of the left-over soup, and slices of bread and liver sausage.

The man with the list joined us in the kitchen, rustling his lists. 'Five sheets of paper, and that's just from this quarter.' He picked up a filled roll from the dresser, then looked at the time and switched the radio on.

The news was relayed to the big bar of the inn, where the people who had just been bombed out raised their heads, waiting to hear the latest bulletin.

The bulletin reported enemy bombers over the Reich, but said that damage had been only slight.

She was tall and very thin, and she coughed a lot. Her eyes were remarkable, extraordinarily striking; they seemed to devour everything they saw.

We met almost nightly in the public air-raid shelter, and sat there side by side, talking, while our exhausted parents dozed on the benches.

The shelter was underneath a large office block, and would hold about five hundred people, but at night only the main room was occupied, and that by some fifty of those who lived near by at the most. There were a number of smaller rooms off the main one, containing camp beds, but they nearly all remained empty.

One night she took my hand and led me to one of these smaller rooms. We huddled there on a straw mattress, side by side, with no one watching, no one to disturb us.

And she talked. As she talked I forgot how tired I was; she told me things she knew, but I could only guess at. Then she coughed again, for an agonizingly long time.

Soon we began meeting outside the air-raid shelter as well. She was a waitress in a café, and I became a regular customer there. Somehow or other, she managed to save her own white bread coupons so that she could get cake with them and let me have it.

At night, when the air-raid warning went, I would go quietly off to our meeting place. She would arrive later and put her arm round my shoulders, press close to me and stroke my hair. I sat beside her, silent and awkward.

Then she coughed into her handkerchief, hiding it afterwards.

As soon as the sirens gave the all-clear we rejoined our parents in the bigger room, and went home to our apartment buildings.

This went on for some weeks, until she was sent away; she had contracted T.B. in the air-raid shelter.

There were at least ten stick-type incendiary bombs burning at various spots scattered through the whole huge office block. We hurried along the corridors with the caretaker; if the master key did not open a door immediately we kicked it in, and if we found an incendiary on the other side we poured sand over it until it was rendered harmless.

There was one room where an artist designed wallpaper patterns in the daytime. Acrid smoke was rising from his paintpots. It was barely possible to reach the source of the smouldering fire at all, and before we could get to the burning stick of the device the ignition charge went off, spreading flames through the whole room. While some of the others stayed to tackle the fire, two of us ran on.

There was another incendiary in what seemed to be a modeller's workshop; it was hissing and spitting sparks. We grabbed the stick and hurled it out of the window into the street. We trampled out the smouldering remnants on the floor, and then looked round the place.

Innumerable pottery figures stood on shelves along the walls, ranged there like objects in a shooting booth: figures of men and women, hares, deer, elephants – crouching, standing, sitting, walking, jumping, dancing. The smallest were only a few centimetres tall, the biggest over half a metre. We forgot about our fire-extinguishing and stopped to look at them, taking them carefully off their shelves to examine them more closely.

Suddenly my companion went back into the middle of the room, and picked up a small lump of clay from the bench. He took aim at the figure of a naked woman standing on tiptoe and waving. She smashed to pieces on the shelf.

'Are you crazy?' I cried.

'Doesn't matter!' he said. 'They'll get compensation for this lot – bomb damage!'

And the pair of us began knocking down the pottery figures along the wall, as if we were competing against each other.

My father put his paper down. 'Wait for your turn,' he said. 'It'll come soon enough. No, I am not signing that paper!'

'But everyone else's parents let them volunteer the moment they're seventeen!' I told him. 'They'll all think I'm a coward!'

'Better to be a coward and keep a whole skin,' said my mother. 'If your friends' parents are crazy, we're not!'

'I'll be so ashamed. When we've won the war I'll be the only one who wasn't in the army,' I grumbled. 'And then what?'

'We haven't won the war yet,' my father pointed out. 'It may take us some time longer! Don't you worry, you'll get your chance to be a soldier.'

'Stay with us, dear!' my mother begged. 'I'm sure I can manage to give you plenty to eat.'

'Out at the front I'd have more to eat than you could possibly get hold of!' I told her. 'Oh, come on, let me go! Do sign!'

'You've seen the casualty lists in the paper every day,' said Mother, very quietly. 'Do you think I want to read *your* name there?'

'Not everyone gets killed!' I said blithely. 'And suppose I

do – why, I might just as easily be killed here in the shelter tonight!'

'You've been reading too many war books,' said my father sarcastically. 'That's right, everyone thinks death only happens to other people – till they get killed themselves. If those who were going to die knew in advance there wouldn't be any wars!'

'You shouldn't say things like that – that's subversion!' I told my father. I repeated, stubbornly, 'But I want to be an officer, and to be an officer you have to have volunteered!'

My father laughed. 'I had a teacher once,' he said, 'who told all the dimmer boys in the class; "You're too stupid for anything else, you'd better join the Army and be lieutenants!" No, you learn a proper trade, that's something you'll be glad of all your life.' Father picked up his paper again. 'And that's that. I'm not signing.'

He signed three weeks later.

In the Barracks

We marched through the town in our best uniforms, singing. Our belts and boots were so shiny they might have been varnished. As we entered the barrack square our song echoed back from the walls of the buildings.

The company commander made us march round the parade ground until we had finished the song, and then ordered us, 'Detachment – halt!' He handed the unit over to the sergeant-major and rode off.

The sergeant-major kept quiet until the officer was out of earshot, waiting till he felt he was on his own before he started in on us.

'Well, we've been preparing you for this day for weeks!' he told us. 'Had to teach you how to march, how to stand at ease, everything. So now you've taken the oath, and I suppose you reckon you're real soldiers because you're about to leave the barracks for the first time . . . well, sworn in or not sworn in, most of you lot don't look good enough to me to show yourselves in uniform out in public! Right, so now I'm going to pick out those of you who don't pass muster!'

We ducked, trying to look as inconspicuous as possible.

The sergeant-major paced along the front rank, scrutinizing every man. 'Helmet crooked! Fall out to the right!' The recruit hesitated.

'I said: "fall out to the right!"' bellowed the sergeant-major.

Biting back his protest, the recruit fell out of the ranks and stood over to one side.

'Button undone! Fall out to the right!' The sergeant-major was singling out almost every other man.

Those who had been fallen out looked enviously at the rest of us.

'Not supposed to show so much tie at the neck! Fall out to the right!' The closer he came, the more worked up the sergeant-major was getting. Now it was my turn for inspection.

I clicked my heels, and tried to look immaculate.

'You swine!' he bellowed at me. 'How dare you take the oath without shaving?'

I said nothing.

'Right, what are you, then?'

'A swine!' I repeated obediently.

'Fall out to the right!'

I did not move. 'Please, sir, permission to explain?'

He looked at me, brows raised.

'I never *have* shaved before.'

The sergeant-major glared at me, obviously quite staggered. 'And you tell me that now?' he said incredulously. He put his hands on his hips. 'Not just a swine – you're a sow!'

'Sir, they didn't issue me with any soap, because I'm still too young.'

He took out his notebook. 'You know, you're going to be sorry you took it upon yourself to tell me my business in front of the whole detachment!' And he wrote my name down. 'Right, fall out!'

I never did get a leave pass the whole time I was a recruit.

The orderly corporal flung open the door, shouting, 'Everybody up!' He waited till we had all jumped out of bed before going on to the next room.

'I think I'll have a lie-in today,' said the man in the bed

next to mine, lying down and pulling up his blankets. 'You go for coffee. I'll follow you.'

At this moment the door opened, and the company commander came in – an unheard of event. He looked round the room and saw my neighbour still lying in bed . . .

My neighbour, horror-struck and unable to move, gazed back at the company commander.

'Are you ill?' snapped the officer.

My neighbour shook his head.

'Then why don't you get up?' shouted the officer.

My neighbour crawled out from under his blankets, trembling with fright.

'What's the idea?' the officer demanded. 'Your name?'

He gave his name, standing there in his nightshirt with his hands down at his sides. Without another word, the company commander left our room, slamming the door behind him.

'That means trouble,' said the room leader. 'Mind you don't put anyone else's back up.'

Before falling in, we all brushed our boots till they shone, cleaned our belts over and over again, and made our beds with exemplary attention to detail. We were ready on the parade ground at the very first whistle.

'What the hell have you been up to?' demanded our section leader. 'The old man's fuming!'

However, before we could explain, the company commander arrived. We returned his 'Good morning!' and saluted.

Then the man who slept next to me was told to step out of the ranks.

'Three days' detention for you, with fatigues!' the company commander told him. 'For failing to obey instantly when the orderly corporal gave orders to get up!'

We were sitting in the room in fatigue dress, hands flat on

our knees, while the corporal instructed us in the correct behaviour of a soldier out in public.

First he recited the ranks we had to salute – a list which ranged from a private to a general in his bathing trunks. Then he tackled the subject of our manners. 'Suppose it's winter. You go out in your overcoat and you're wearing gloves. What's that, eh?' He jerked his chin towards a recruit sitting directly in front of him.

The recruit got up and looked helplessly round at the rest of us. Suddenly he had an inspiration. 'Regulation winter uniform, sir!'

'Wrong!' barked the corporal. 'The action of a coward, that's what it is! You shouldn't have any gloves! All gloves belong with our comrades freezing on the Eastern front, see?'

'Yes, sir!' said the recruit, sitting down again.

'However, let's suppose you *do* go out with gloves on,' the corporal went on. 'And you meet your girl friend, who offers you her hand. So what do you do then?' He pointed to someone at the back. 'You – you were a university student! I suppose *you* know the way to behave?'

The lad addressed jumped up. 'Oh, yes, sir! I take off my glove before I shake her hand!'

'Wrong!' bellowed the corporal. He laughed, raucously. 'Huh! So much for all this education! You do no such thing! You keep your glove on. Your gloves are as much part of your uniform as your trousers, and you're not going to take your trousers off when you see your girl friend – or are you, then? Ho, ho, ho . . .' chuckled the corporal.

The ex-student went scarlet and sat down.

After the corporal had finished laughing, he went on. 'Now, what do you do when you're in a bar and you get into a quarrel with a civilian?'

We had no idea.

'Well, first you take the fellow outside, so you don't have such a large audience. As you know, people are going to take more notice of you when you're in uniform; you represent the Army. But once you're outside the place, this filthy civilian insults your uniform – maybe he even hits you. Then what?'

An arm went up in the front row.

'Right – you!'

'I defend myself!' said the recruit.

'Defend yourself . . . !' repeated the corporal, sarcastically. 'Defend yourself! This oaf has insulted the honour of the Army, and surely you know that a stain on your honour can only be wiped out with blood? What you do is kill the filthy swine! Make sure he's good and dead, though, or he may end up in court giving evidence against you.'

At noon we always came back from our duty spell of work on the land worn out, with the knees of our trousers wet and muddy. Covered with dirt, but singing, we marched in through the barracks gate.

When we were dismissed there was a rush for dinner. The swiftest got to the front of the queue for food, while the strongest pushed their way in.

We ate fast, because if you finished your meal quickly enough you could get a place in the washroom. Most of us spent our dinner hour there, running basins full of water to wash our breeches, and scrubbing at the dirty marks on them with a stiff brush. However, if you were late you would find the washroom occupied, and then you had to wash your trousers when you came off duty in the evening, while the others went out. The last men were still hard at it in the washroom late at night.

We rigged up a line from corner to corner of our room, and hung our dripping trousers up to dry. We always competed for a place by the window, feeling that the breeches would dry faster there. But whether they were washed at dinner time or in the evening, whether they were hung by the window or in the far corner, they never did get dry; the material was too thick, and the time between one duty spell of work on the land and the next too short.

Sometimes we even lit the stove in the evenings, which was forbidden, in the hope of getting our trousers dry, and then we had to put up with sleeping in the damp heat of the room on a summer night. The orderly corporal would wrinkle his nose at the smell next morning. As for us, we would climb into our stiff breeches, still so damp that we were chilled to the bone in them even in the summer sun, and go out for our next spell on the land in clammy but clean trousers.

We had been watching the show going on in the barrack square for about an hour, grinding our teeth as we looked out of our room window.

Down there, the section leader was 'licking into shape', as he put it, the toughest man in our room, for dropping his rifle during drill.

Our friend down there was a short man, but sturdy and so strong that he could carry two of us on his back at once. Now, however, he was dragging himself wearily across the sand of the barrack square, knees bent.

The corporal, dressed to go out, was standing at the edge of the square, hands on his hips, shouting orders at our friend. He hardly moved, for fear of taking any of the gloss off his highly polished boots.

Our friend had to crawl over the ground like a seal. Sweat and dirt plastered his tunic, and his face was filthy. He lay there helpless and exhausted for a moment or two, until the corporal's voice brought him to his feet again.

The corporal ended the session on the dot of the hour, dismissed the culprit, turned smartly on his heel and left the barracks.

Our friend stood alone in the middle of the big square for a minute, tried to take a step, swayed and fell. We ran out and picked him up; he was quite unable to walk. Four of us carried him into the room and laid him on his bed.

His eyes were closed, and he was groaning; his usually ruddy face was pale. We took off his boots and undressed him, went to the washroom to dip some handkerchiefs in water, and put them on his chest and forehead.

Gradually, he recovered consciousness. He looked around him and then, suddenly, began to cry like a child, clenching his fists. Through his tears he uttered, between his teeth, 'The brute! The brute!' He kept on and on repeating it, fury in his voice.

We tried to calm him down. All of a sudden he sat up in bed, leaning on one elbow, and looked round at us. 'If I ever run into that bastard at the front, I'm going to shoot him!' he said, loud and very clear.

Ties were in one pile, shirts in another, underpants in another – all brand new.

We stood in a long queue by the shelves; we could have helped ourselves from the stacks of clothes just by stretching out an arm. However, the storekeeper kept a sharp eye on his supplies. He was watching us the whole time, and never turned his back.

Our queue advanced slowly towards the end of the room, where a solitary clerk sat behind a table, keeping careful records. He wrote a list of the garments issued beside our names, and then entered them in our paybooks. Finally he issued everyone with a woollen abdominal belt as winter equipment.

I was looking for the shelf with singlets on it.

'Sir,' the clerk called out, 'according to his paybook, this man's already got an abdominal belt.'

'No, I haven't,' said the soldier. 'Must have been entered by mistake. I've never had one.'

'Let's have a look at your paybook,' said the storekeeper, moving two or three paces away from his place to examine the page of entries.

We were on the alert in a flash. The first man grabbed three hand-towels and stuffed them down the waistband of his trousers. I still hadn't found any singlets. The man in front of me made for a pile of socks, but instead of picking up a pair he pulled a whole bundle off the shelf. He stood there transfixed and horrified, holding the bulky bundle. Someone or other pulled off the string round it, and twelve pairs of grey socks fell to the floor. Before the storekeeper could raise his head they had all disappeared down the tops of boots, into trouser pockets, under fatigue jackets.

After supper, I swopped two pairs of new woollen socks for two new singlets with another man.

For days it had been so cold that we could hardly sleep under our two blankets. In the evening, when I was on room duties, I swept the room out with special care, dusted all the surfaces, even tidied the other men's clothes into neater piles. Then I lit the stove.

The orderly corporal was inspecting our corridor, room by room. He was getting closer now . . . two rooms away . . . the room next door . . .

The door was flung open. Steel helmet on his head, there stood the orderly corporal, waiting for my report.

I duly recited the correct formula. The corporal examined my clothes. Finding nothing to object to, he walked suspiciously over to the window between the bunk beds. All the others were awake, but they pretended to be asleep.

The corporal ran his forefinger below the window sill, and then examined it. 'Hm, well!' he said.

I breathed a sigh of relief.

As he went out he inspected a cupboard; in so doing he came close to the stove. He stopped in surprise, turned, and suddenly took the lid off the stove. 'Aha!' he said, pleased. 'Why isn't this fire out?' he shouted at me.

All the 'sleeping' men were watching me and the corporal through half-closed eyes.

'We were cold . . .' I explained.

'Don't you know the rules? All fires to be out and all stoves emptied at curfew time, because of fire risk and on hygienic grounds,' he said cuttingly.

'Yes, sir!'

Slowly, he opened the stove and pulled out the ash drawer, and then walked deliberately through the room, scattering its contents evenly over the floor. Sparks jumped across the tiles and dust filled the air. We all began to cough.

He dropped the ash drawer with the remaining ashes in the middle of the room and made his own getaway. I was left there among the ashes and dust, coughing. The orderly corporal peered in again through a crack in the door. 'And you're not going to bed until this room is spotless!' he shouted at me.

My boots were new. I had spent hours rubbing grease into them until the leather was soft, because once that was done they would mould themselves to the foot and never pinch, even after a long march.

We were given a briefing, and I was told to report to the orderly room after boot inspection. The N.C.O. on duty inspected every boot thoroughly. If he felt the vamp was too hard, or found any dirt in between the nails on the sole, or considered the seam of the leg was not white enough, he would send the culprit up to his room to repair the omission.

My boots passed muster.

When he could find nothing more to criticize, we had to tie each pair of boots together with a piece of string and take them to the clothing store.

'Please, sir, can I keep my boots?' I asked. 'I'm being transferred to instruction courses this week.'

He refused. 'My orders were: all boots back to the store!'

After roll-call I reported to the sergeant-major wearing lace-up shoes.

'Where are your boots?' snapped the sergeant-major.

'Took them back to the store, sir!' I said.

'You fool, you knew you were going on instruction courses! Leaving tonight! So now I suppose we've got to open up the store all over again, just for you!'

The N.C.O. who had inspected my boots spluttered with fury. 'You great oaf, why couldn't you have said so before? He directed me to the pile of boots we had handed in. 'Find yourself a pair, then, and get a move on! I've got a date!'

I searched and searched, and went on searching until he threw me out, but I didn't find my own pair of boots.

The corporal inspected me from head to foot. I could tell just from his face, that he didn't like me. 'Right, so you're in my section!' he said. 'Candidate for a commission, eh?' He came so close I could feel his breath on my face. 'Are we allowed to touch?' he said sweetly.

'Yes, sir!'

Taking hold of the button on my left breast pocket, he tore it off in a single movement. 'Coming on parade with pocket unbuttoned . . . oh, I like that, I really do!' he said, grinning

He took three steps backwards with my button in his hand, took aim, and tossed it down on the ground in front of me. 'Get down flat beside that button!' he shouted.

I stepped out of line and duly lay flat beside the button.

'Advance!' ordered the corporal.

Gripping my rifle in both hands, I worked my way forward on elbows and knees over the damp sand. I crossed the whole square in this position.

'About turn!' he shouted.

I went back the same way.

'Stand to attention!'

My eyes on the corporal, I jumped up and stood to attention. My uniform was plastered with sand.

'Let's see your rifle!'

I swung up my rifle and held it out to him.

'The barrel; I want to see the barrel!' he demanded.

Muzzle protector off, lock out, rifle held up . . .

He peered down the barrel. 'Sand!' he bellowed. 'You've got sand down that barrel! That's the way you treat your weapon, is it?' He made me reassemble the gun, and then sent me off over the parade ground.

I had to march and run and hop and crawl; I had to dig myself in, and practise rifle drill . . .

After half an hour of this, he stationed me in front of the rest of the section. My helmet was askew, my hair was sticking to my forehead, and sweat ran down my face. I was panting. My tie hung out from my collar, and whenever I moved the sand trickled out of my uniform. My hands were trembling so violently that I could hardly hold my gun, and I was no longer able to keep my knees together.

The corporal hooted with laughter. He slapped his thigh. 'What a sissy! And he wants to be an officer! I ask you!'

*

'Now, if you've dug your slit-hole deep enough, and if you act correctly, you'll find that the tanks will pass overhead quite safely,' the lieutenant told us.

We stared at the hole at our feet. It was as deep as the height of a man, and broad enough to accommodate a pair of shoulders.

'This is a correctly dug slit-hole,' our instructor assured us. 'So who feels like going first?'

One of the section volunteered, got into the hole and crouched down. The lieutenant gave him a few more directions, and even handed him a ground sheet to keep off the falling dirt. He waited till the volunteer was in position, and then ordered us back.

At a gesture of command from him, the crew got into the small, old tank, closing all its doors, and the engine began to race. Ponderously, the dilapidated vehicle started moving. We grinned as we watched it.

It made its way forward, until its right track was exactly above the slit-hole – and stuck there, while the left track went on running. Slowly and noisily, the tank swivelled above the slit-hole, grinding its way into the sandy soil, sinking deeper and deeper in.

Suddenly a piercing shriek rose above the noise the tank was making, a sound that went on and on, shrill and agonizing.

The lieutenant waved his arms frantically. The turret door opened, and the tank did another half turn before lurching away from the hole.

We had some difficulty in getting our companion out of the debris in the correctly dug slit-hole. He was unconscious, his right arm crushed, a bloody mess of bone splinters, torn flesh and rags of uniform.

The instructor gave the man-sized straw dummy a friendly slap on the shoulder. 'And now for our friend here! We'll see about slitting his stomach open for him!' he said amiably, adding sharply, 'Fix bayonets!'

Each of us whipped out the shiny blade and thrust it into the bayonet holder of the rifle until the locking pin was in place. The corporal instructing us took the gun from one member of the section and demonstrated hand-to-hand fighting. 'No stabbing,' he told us. 'You fall towards your enemy with your bayonet fixed, and when it's right in, then you turn the butt end of the gun outwards.'

Our faces twitched as we watched his demonstration, and we swallowed painfully.

'Then, as soon as you've twisted the bayonet in his stomach, get it out again. Finally you ram the butt into his mouth, and that should do it. And on you go to the next. Get the idea?'

'Yes, sir!' we chorused.

He nodded, satisfied. 'Then let's begin.'

One by one, we ran at the straw dummy, plunging the blade in and smashing it with the butt of the rifle. The corporal stood and watched, urging us on with shouts of, 'At him! Get right in there now! Harder!' We went on practising until the straw dummy had completely disintegrated.

'Good! Well done!' our instructor praised us. 'Now, get into a semi-circle.'

The section stationed itself round him in a semi-circle.

'And now for the finer points of hand-to-hand fighting,' he told us, grinning. 'That straw dummy doesn't tell you the whole of it – in actual fact you'll have to thrust much harder. The fellow facing you may be wearing three pairs of underpants, and you've got to get through the lot. And once you've finished, you're left with him hanging on your rifle like a stuck pig. So the trick is, once you've thrust at him, you need

41

to give him a kick in the balls, and that'll free your weapon for the next man.'

'I was first to get changed today!' said the man who had been sitting beside me at dinner. While the rest of us were dashing from the table to our own quarters, to get our trousers off and change into riding breeches, this man had simply tucked his ordinary trousers into the boots he was wearing. This made the trousers balloon out slightly at the sides, above his knees, so that they did look quite like riding breeches.

Our riding instructor merely grinned when he saw my dinner-time companion in his improvised riding breeches, and allotted him the most unreliable horse, one we all feared getting. Then he told us to mount.

The horses walked quietly round the riding school, obeying only the instructor, and keeping close together. Once we had ridden round a few times, the instructor told the horses, 'Trot!' and they immediately began to trot, going faster. If you did not accommodate yourself to their movements you got a thorough shaking. My dinner-time companion was just ahead of me. I looked at his legs, and saw that the long trousers were gradually creeping up out of his boots; however much he slid back and forth in the saddle, his trouser-legs worked their way up higher and higher.

The riding instructor, arms folded, stood in the middle of the hall watching us.

The horses trotted round and round in the sawdust. My companion's trousers were like a thick ring around his thighs, and now his long white underpants were beginning to ride up too. His face twisted with pain, he crouched on his animal. Still keeping up the pace, the horses trotted on.

The field-grey trousers and white underpants had now merged into two rolls of cloth, each as thick as an arm, and underneath them blood ran down the man's naked legs and into the tops of his boots.

He clung desperately to his saddle, no longer capable of riding properly, as his horse jerked him back and forth. But the ride went on. Gradually, all that was visible of the white underpants was dyed red. The rider lay on his horse now, clinging to its mane for dear life.

Only then did the instructor stop the horses. Groaning, the bloodstained man tumbled off his animal.

'And what will *you* be wearing for the next riding lesson?' asked the instructor.

'Riding breeches, sir!' said my companion.

'Go and straighten out your clothes at once!' the instructor ordered. 'I want to get this riding lesson started.'

Before they sent us to the front we went home on leave.

I stopped at the place where our building used to stand on my way from the station to my grandfather's little house. There were piles of rubble on every side, but the façade of our building was still there, with gaping, empty holes where the windows used to be. The only bit of window frame left was in what used to be my room; there was nothing at all behind it. Rubble overflowed from the door of the building and out on to the pavement.

My grandfather's house was still undamaged, and there was a room in the attic where my mother slept among all the things she had been able to salvage from our belongings. My father had been called up.

Grandmother gave me a warm welcome, but almost immediately she began to look worried. She went to a cupboard and produced a bundle of ration cards with nearly all the coupons cut out. 'I can't offer you anything to eat!' she said. 'This is all we have left.'

43

Looking at the clock, I asked her where the nearest ration card distribution centre was. I had to run to get there in time, and I was the last to get my special leave coupons that day, so that when I got back the shops were closed. Grandmother took my coupons and added them to her own bundle of ration cards. Then I waited.

It was getting dark when my mother came home from work; she had been drafted into the war effort when Father was called up. Grandfather too had come out of retirement and was back at work. He came home even later.

At last we sat down at the table. There were baked potatoes, and everyone had a slice of bread and marmalade; there was potato in the bread too. I had to tell the family about everything I had been doing. They sat there listening, yawning now and then. And we kept our ears pricked for an air-raid warning.

On the last day of my leave I went with my mother to the administrative offices where she was working. I had to hand over my paybook and sign an undertaking of secrecy before I was allowed into the building.

The head of my mother's department seemed friendly. He welcomed us both, shook my hand, and called me 'comrade'. Then he asked what we wanted.

My mother asked for the next day off work, so that she could see me off at the station.

'You're off to the front, are you?' asked my mother's boss. 'This is your last leave before you go?'

I said it was.

He drew breath in audibly through his nose, and shook his head thoughtfully. 'I'm sure you know how essential our work is to the war effort,' he began. 'I could quote that saying about every hour of work missed delaying the final victory . . . and so forth. Well, the fact is, I can't give people days off.' He scratched the lobe of one ear with his forefinger. 'What time does your train leave?'

'Ten-thirty.'

'In that case,' he said, turning to my mother, 'you could be back at work by eleven-thirty at the latest – that's allowing for possible delays, and the tram ride.' He heaved a sigh of relief. 'I don't mind taking responsibility for that. But don't let me down, will you?' And he got up. 'Well, back to work!' He shook hands with me again, and wished me luck.

My mother went off to her own work, and one of the other staff showed me out of the building.

I wandered aimlessly round the town on my own, stopping to look at ruins and piles of rubble and wonder what used to stand there. I found a café, its broken plate-glass windows replaced by boards, where soldiers on leave could have a piece of cake without producing coupons. I ate my piece and washed it down with a cup of substitute coffee. The waitress marked my pass with indelible pencil and a rubber stamp, to show that I had had my piece of cake and prevent me from getting another.

We reached the station about ten o'clock. I had a parcel containing a cake attached to my luggage; Grandmother had baked it as a farewell present. Mother had washed and ironed the last of my dirty clothes overnight.

There were soldiers waiting on the platform, their rucksacks on their backs, with wives and mothers, red-eyed from crying, standing beside them. Along with them waited people who had been bombed out, their last few possessions in cardboard boxes at their feet.

An officer was pacing restlessly up and down the platform, responding inattentively to the soldiers' salutes; they had to keep on saluting him again.

My mother was looking at me, saying nothing. I couldn't think of anything to say either. I kept glancing the way the train would come in.

'Are you sure you haven't forgotten anything?' Mother asked. She had asked the same question three times already.

I ran over the list for the third time. 'Towel, soap, shirts, ties . . .'

Suddenly my mother darted off and returned with a newspaper. 'To read on the journey,' she explained.

I thanked her, and wedged the paper in between my back and my rucksack. Mother was fiddling with her handbag. 'I'm sure you haven't got enough handkerchiefs! Here, take this one.'

'No, I've got plenty!' I assured her.

'Do take it!' Mother begged me. 'You can always do with an extra handkerchief!' She put it into my pocket.

By now the clock was showing 10.40. The station-master walked up the platform, calling, 'The train that was due to depart at 10.32 is expected to be over an hour late!'

'Why?' asked the officer.

'Must have been diverted,' said the station-master. 'The line was bombed again last night.'

Mother looked at the station clock, trying to do it surreptitiously so that I wouldn't notice. She was obviously getting worried; she stood there shifting her handbag from hand to hand. We were silent again. I took Mother's arm and led her to the end of the platform. Her glances at the station clock were getting more frequent now. 'Nearly eleven!' she whispered.

'Would you rather go?' I asked.

She shook her head, but in a moment she said, under her breath, 'I don't want to let him down.'

'You go!' I told her. 'Heaven knows how much longer it may be!'

She hesitated, her eyes going from the clock to me, and back to the clock, and back to me again. Without meaning to, she was drawing me in the direction of the barrier.

'Yes, you go now!' I said. 'Or perhaps he won't give you a couple of hours off next time!'

She nodded, crying; she kissed me, hugged me, tore herself away. She waved, and then came back, and went again. Now she was out of sight . . . and there was still so much I wanted to say to her.

At the Front

The train journey had lasted two days and two nights, and there were at least two more days and nights to come. Frozen and tired out, I accepted a mug of weak tea from a bleary-eyed Red Cross sister. It tasted revolting, but at least it was hot.

There was an iron stove as tall as a man in the middle of the hut. It was stuffed with railway coal. It glowed deep red, and roared, and white sparks shot out of the red-hot stovepipe whenever anyone raked out the ashes.

I drew up a stool as close to this monster as I could get. Steam rose from my damp battledress blouse as I drank my tea in small sips, warming my hands on the mug. When I got too hot on the side nearest the stove, I turned my back to the heat. I was dead tired. After a while I turned round to warm my front. I put the mug down, and sleep overcame me . . .

. . . Once again the train was shaking me as it rattled on; villages were whisking past, forests, endless fields, bridges, towns, stations, Red Cross nursing sisters with big cans of coffee, and then more woods, fields, snow, vast expanses of snow, and in front of it all the telegraph poles, poles with wires seeming to rise and fall, countless poles, never-ending wires, dirty windows, dirty corridors, sliding doors that stuck, compartments full of soldiers, rather smelly, rucksacks in the luggage nets, and cardboard boxes, and a huge red and black case, an extremely large case shifting slowly forward, coming closer, beginning to tip over the edge . . .

I tried to catch and hold it; I fell, and in falling knocked my head against the glowing stove. The mug was knocked over and my tea spilled on the side of the stove, hissing. My forehead struck the open ash-trap.

My cap was singed.

We were dragging tree trunks up to the bunker we were building, in groups of seven. Steel helmets not to be removed during work were our orders. We couldn't hear any shots; we sweated and grumbled, but the order was not countermanded.

With the heavy weights we were carrying it was hard going through the woods, where the ground was often marshy. We all had to carry the tree trunk on the same shoulder; the last man in line was the one who decided which shoulder.

I was walking last in a party carrying a tree trunk at least five metres long and almost half a metre thick. My steel helmet was digging into my head, my shoulder hurt, and I felt it was time for a change. I carefully wriggled my head round to the other side of the trunk, so that its weight was on my other shoulder. Then I called, 'Change shoulders!'

At the same moment two or three bursts of mortar fire rang out.

No one did change shoulders; with one accord, they dropped the tree trunk, flinging it aside – to the side my head was on.

The trunk pulled me to the ground as it fell, passing over my steel helmet, dropping with a muffled thud, and then trundling on until it reached an old, half rotted tree stump. Far off, shells were bursting.

I lay on the ground as if stunned, listening quite indifferently to fresh bursts of firing. Rather reluctantly, the others came out of cover, gathered round and stared down at me.

When I tried standing up, I found my knees were trembling. Someone undid my steel helmet for me. It was badly dented.

Our section was advancing through the forest, checking the area, when we found the fallen man in the undergrowth.

He was lying on the moss, eyes closed as if asleep, smiling slightly. His foreign uniform was hardly even dirty.

'He's not been here long,' said the lance-corporal leading us.

'And look at those boots!' said the man just behind him. 'Russian leather! Practically new, too!' He bent over the dead man, handling the leather. 'Feel that! Soft, eh?'

The lance-corporal agreed without bothering to bend down. 'Better than our old clodhoppers by a long way!' He lit a cigarette.

We were all standing round the corpse. Suddenly, the private who had admired the boots handed his gun to another man, sat down on the ground and placed the soles of his feet against those of the dead man.

'My size, too!' he said. 'I'm going to have those boots!'

'Leave them alone!' someone warned him. 'If that lot over there catch you with them, they'll kill us all!'

'Oh, rubbish!' said the private. He stood up and began pulling at the leather boots. However, they refused to come off. The corpse slid along the ground.

'Hold on to him, will you?' the private asked the lance-corporal. Submachine gun in one hand, lighted cigarette in the other, the lance-corporal simply placed his foot on the corpse's stomach, and the private went on pulling.

'Trying to pull his leg off?' someone asked.

'We'll have to break his legs, or I'll never get 'em off!' said the private.

'Don't be a fool – there's no time for that!' growled the lance-corporal. Angrily, the private dropped the dead man's leg again and took back the gun, venting his annoyance by kicking the corpse.

The lance-corporal raised his hand, and we started off again. The private looked back at the fallen man once more. 'What a shame!' he said, regretfully. 'What a shame about those beautiful boots!'

'Call this a bunker!' grunted the platoon leader. He put a hand up to the roof. 'Nothing but a layer of planks!' he complained. 'Those swine were too lazy to build us a good solid bunker – might have expected as much!' Then he opened the door. He made no comment, simply shook his head.

The bunker contained nothing, nothing at all; no floor, no camp beds. It was empty, set down on the bare ground.

After a long pause, the sergeant heaved a loud sigh. But it was getting dark by now, and we had to move in. Three men fetched some twigs from the near-by bushes and spread them on the floor of the bunker. We laid our haversacks and combat packs down in a row by the longer wall, to act as pillows. There were only twelve men in our platoon, but still the place was not really long enough to hold us all.

'It'll just have to do,' said the platoon leader.

We all had another piece of bread and honey spread, and then night fell. One by one we crawled into the bunker. We had to sleep on our sides if everyone was to have room.

The sergeant was the last to come in, and had to push his way into the row of men. He managed it, though with a certain amount of swearing.

'Don't curl your legs up like that!' someone in the corner grumbled.

'You fool, what else can I do?' snorted the sergeant. 'There isn't room to stretch my legs out – this place is too narrow!'

However, we soon fell asleep, and I did not wake till it was time to turn over. Someone wanted to change sides, which was possible only if everyone else changed sides too.

I woke for the second time to hear firing very close to us. The bunker itself swayed, waking everyone.

'Get out of here – this is a mass grave!' yelled the platoon leader.

One by one, we crawled out into the open, dispersed around the terrain and waited, still drowsy, for the end of the attack.

Suddenly the sergeant let out an infuriated bellow. 'And they call this a rest area!'

I left the ration of brandy allocated to me, and instead took my bar of chocolate off to a small clearing. I could hear the singing from inside the bunker. Sporadic rifle shots were falling in our lines, and sometimes there were short bursts of rattling machine-gun fire.

I took off my shirt and let the early spring sun shine on my naked chest. While I ate my chocolate, I picked lice out of my shirt and squashed them.

Suddenly I saw the platoon leader in front of me, his face scarlet. 'Come along, you!' he said. His breath smelled of brandy.

The entire platoon was sitting in the bunker, singing and drinking. When they saw me they grinned and fell silent.

'Give us your mug, then!' said the sergeant.

I had rather a pretty mug, pale blue outside and white inside, containing exactly two centilitres. I got it out of my pack, and the platoon leader took it from me. 'Here – that's your ration!' he said, holding up the bottle. He filled my mug to the brim. 'Everyone in this platoon must join in the drinking!' He roared with laughter, and pressed the mug into my hand. 'So you just drink that up!'

They were all looking at me.

The mere idea of the brandy turned my stomach. Reluctantly, I put it to my lips.

'Come on, drink up!'

It tasted horribly bitter. After the first sip I felt like . . .

'Get it down in one!' bawled the sergeant.

I swallowed it somehow. It left me shaking, but finally the mug was empty. 'Mission accomplished!' I announced.

'Good!' said the sergeant, satisfied. 'I don't stand for any dodgers in my platoon,' he told us. 'Red-blooded men, that's what I want, see?' He laughed sardonically. 'If you want to be an officer, you have to set a good example in everything. Drinking included!'

'Yes, sir!' I groaned. The mug dropped from my hand, and I vomited right in the middle of the bunker.

I was standing by the wooden camouflage screen that sheltered us from observation and enemy fire, right beside the gap. There were about thirty metres of the screen missing at this point, a gap which meant one had to go a long way round – a diversion of almost three hundred metres. Three hundred metres over boggy ground . . .

I thought I might as well save myself taking the long way round. I ran. Ten steps, fifteen . . . before I was halfway across the gap I felt something thud into my back, and knew at once that I had been hit, though I still felt no pain. I ran on, and as I ran I saw blood spurt from the upper part of my left arm. Suddenly I couldn't breathe.

Behind the screen, the others picked me up.

'Well, congratulations!' said the lance-corporal. 'That'll get you sent home all right!'

'Snipers!' said the sergeant. He was getting my blouse and shirt off me. 'You were lucky it wasn't a shell.'

It only began to hurt when the medical orderly put a

tourniquet on the artery. 'Right through the lung and the upper arm,' he said, covering the entry hole in my back with an air-proof plaster. 'Over to the right a bit, and it'd have gone through your backbone and your heart.'

'Is the bone damaged?' I asked.

The orderly looked; I bit back the pain as he examined me. Then he shook his head.

'Oh, hell!' I grumbled. 'It'll take me ages to get my lieutenant's commission now!'

'I dare say you'll make it soon enough!' said the sergeant, without much sympathy.

Then they strapped me to a stretcher and carried me back behind the lines.

I had been lying by the track on my stretcher for hours, crying, beside myself with pain. There was an anti-tank gun crew in position about a hundred metres off. One member of the gun crew, a private, came over to me.

'Untie my arm!' I yelled at him.

He bent over me and loosened the knot. The blood spurted up, and I groaned out loud in relief.

'Hey, this looks bad to me!' said the man. 'I'm no expert at this kind of thing!' And he hastily did the arm up again.

I pleaded with him, shouting and writhing and tossing my head from side to side.

'Hang on, the ambulance will be here soon,' he said as he went away, trying to give me courage.

I lay there in the sun, crying. My arm, with the tight tourniquet on it, was getting more swollen now, and beginning to turn blue. I was in dreadful pain; I bawled until my voice gave out. But no other member of the gun crew came over to me.

At last the ambulance with its red cross on the side drove

up, and the driver climbed wearily out of his seat. His uniform was covered with bloodstains. He picked up the head end of my stretcher and dragged me into his vehicle.

Someone was whimpering up above my head. The door slammed shut; the ambulance started off, jolting slowly along the corduroy road. The man above me screamed like an animal. I was flung from side to side on my stretcher, and found myself uttering piercing screams too.

The ambulance jolted on, faster now, and the wounded man above me was in a frenzy. We both howled in unison. Then the ambulance stopped and the door opened. I saw a doctor wearing a butcher's apron and talking to the tired driver, who was explaining, 'The man on top has about thirty splinters in him – but you'll have to deal with the bottom one first; he's got a tourniquet on.'

Wounded

The bunker stank of blood and pus. I lay strapped to a rickety operating table, while the doctor, with his back to me, told an orderly what to put on the record card. All I caught was the fragment of a sentence.

'. . . never save that arm . . .'

Then the doctor turned to look at me.

I begged, I prayed. He merely shrugged his shoulders. I tried to pull free. Then he snapped at me. 'Listen, there are other people waiting for their turn too!'

They put an injection in my arm, and an orderly in a vile-smelling battledress blouse held my head. I felt a sudden sensation like a pencil being drawn across my wounded arm. I tried to look, but the orderly forced my head over to the other side.

The doctor began to saw.

It did not hurt, though my head was vibrating, my feet trembling, and everything about me was quivering. I bellowed like an animal. The orderly leaned his whole weight against my head, and I felt someone throw himself across my legs.

Suddenly it was all over, and they let go of me. I felt as if I were floating in the air.

Another orderly of some kind came up to the operating table with a dirty old crate that had held ammunition. I was just in time to see the doctor toss my arm into it . . .

There were wounded men in the auditorium and on the stage; the whole theatre had been turned into a hospital. The theatre people themselves had been pressed into service, and girls who used to be ballet dancers were now working as cleaners.

There were six beds in what was once an actor's dressing-room. I was in one of them, along with a man who had lost a leg and four minor casualties. We had only one topic of conversation between us: the Russian girl who came to clean out our room every morning.

It was hot, sultry weather. A battalion of Russian auxiliaries were marching up and down the square outside our window, singing their plaintive songs. After the doctor's visit we began staring as if spell-bound at the door, waiting for the Russian girl.

One of the minor casualties got up and peered along the corridor. At last she arrived, smiled, gave us a guttural 'Good morning!' and put her bucket and scrubbing brush down.

The man who had been standing by the door limped towards his bed, thus forcing her into the middle of the room. Suddenly he threw her on the empty bed.

In an instant we were all alert; even the one-legged man sat up in bed.

The Russian girl was quite silent, though she fought desperately. Even while defending herself she took care not to hit out at anyone's wounds. We could hear the uneven, frantic breathing in the room louder than the singing outside. There was a sound of something tearing . . .

Footsteps.

The Russian girl pushed us all away from her, and we scuttled back to our beds. She pulled her torn dress together over her breasts with her left hand, picked up her scrubbing brush and bucket and went out. She said, 'Auf wiedersehen!' just as usual at the door.

But we never did see her again.

We filled the great hall, bed beside bed, at least twenty in a row, and there were four rows. There was hardly any room left for bedside lockers.

Those of us by the windows could watch children playing and women going shopping on the other side of the wall. The rest could only see other wounded men, and beds with uniforms hanging at their heads and temperature charts at their feet.

The airman to my right had broken his back jumping from his burning plane; the gunner to my left had lost both feet from frostbite. My neighbours did not talk much, though one sometimes heard a suppressed curse when the armoured infantry rifleman was going on again.

This man's bed was diagonally opposite mine. He had been shot in the head, and he never seemed to stop talking. He began when they took our temperatures first thing in the morning and went on until evening, stopping only when we threatened to throw him out of the window.

One afternoon the orderly-room clerk came over to my bed. 'I need your paybook,' he told me. He sat down by the rifleman to listen.

As I got out my paybook, the rifleman was rambling on about a certain sergeant in his unit, talking so loud that everyone could hear. '. . . yes, when he heard those first shells he wanted to get out of there! But he got caught in the barbed wire – tore his trousers. He got a great scratch down one calf, so that was his first wound. Then he was wounded for the second time, even before they gave him his black stripe for the first wound. He was standing near a machine gun delivering harassing fire, and the gunner had to change the barrel because one shell case got stuck. The red-hot barrel flew aside and landed on our sergeant's feet. He had blisters as big as walnuts. A couple of days later there was some shrapnel about the place – it got a man standing just in front of the sergeant, and this fellow toppled over, hit the sergeant's foot with the edge of his steel helmet and broke his little toe. So that was the sergeant's third wound in four days. The C.O. in person presented him with his silver stripe and the Iron Cross, Second Class!'

The orderly-room clerk laughed and slapped the rifleman's shoulder. Then he took my paybook and went out, as the rifleman began on his next story.

He came back half an hour later, and threw my paybook and a small cardboard box on the bedspread. 'Congratulations!' he said, turning to go.

The cardboard box contained my own silver stripe and the Iron Cross, Second Class.

The more able-bodied of us decorated the little hall. Every inmate of the hospital was issued with clean blue-and-white striped pyjamas. We were to have a show given by performers who went round entertaining the troops.

I had to go for massage on the afternoon of the performance, and when I came back the show had already begun. We were supposed to be in hospital wear, but though I was in uniform the staff doctor allowed me in, and even made a way for me to get through the rows of seats. I found a seat right in the middle of the front row, and there I sat, the only man in uniform among the striped blue-and-white figures.

An elderly and rather stout man was singing some Schubert songs, very loud. Next came a conjuror, who was followed by a pianist playing a rhapsody by Liszt. There was a contortionist who put her head between her knees backwards, and went around the stage like that.

The next turn was a woman singing popular hit songs. We duly applauded as she came on. Her glance fell on me in my uniform. I thought it was just chance until she got to the chorus, but then she looked straight at me as she sang.

'Peter, dear Peter, oh, what have you done?

I can't rest, by night or day . . .'

To left and right of me, the others grinned, and someone nudged me. I went scarlet and hunched up my shoulders.

But she was still singing directly at me.

'Peter, dear Peter, I'll never forget you,

Come what may . . .'

There were appreciative murmurs behind me. I felt like crawling away to hide. She put a lot of feeling into the words, and finally, coming down from the stage, she came quite close, leaned over me, and breathed the final lines of her song very quietly.

'I will give you anything –

I'll give myself to you.'

The audience stamped their feet and cheered. This was the high spot of the show! As the singer climbed back on stage she blew me a parting kiss.

The staff doctor called me over to him. 'Now then, corporal, do your stuff!' he said. He got the nurses to pick flowers from the hospital garden and make up a huge bouquet for me, and after the performance I took this bouquet to the singer's dressing-room and knocked, timidly.

She opened the door herself and accepted the flowers. I stood there waiting.

'You didn't take any of that seriously, I hope, young man?' she said. 'It's all in the day's work, you know! So long!'

The man whose leg had been amputated at the thigh limped along beside me, leaning on my shoulder. The doctor stopped once again at the door and turned to us. 'Don't let me down, will you?' he said quietly. Then he turned the handle.

The young soldier was lying by a window with a view of the garden. His breakfast, untouched, stood on the locker beside him.

'Here, I've brought a couple of friends to see you,' said the doctor with brisk cheerfulness, sitting on the bed. 'They're in the same boat too!''

The young soldier did not even turn his head towards us. He was staring at the ceiling. But the doctor pressed on. 'Look at *him*.' He pointed to the one-legged man. 'Could be your father! We've taken his whole leg off – and now he's hopping around the place all day, manages the stairs and everything!'

The young soldier still did not move.

'And then there's this young fellow!' The doctor clapped me on the left shoulder. 'He's only got one arm, but you should just see him swim! He's hardly any older than you, either!'

The young soldier's mouth began to tremble, and his eyes slowly filled with tears. He sobbed.

'Of course it was bad luck that mine took the lower part of your leg off,' the doctor said. 'But there's nothing else the matter with you, nothing at all. You'll soon get over it. At your age the wound will heal quickly, and you'll get a good artificial limb – you'll even be able to dance with it . . .'

'It doesn't make sense,' muttered the young soldier, in agony. 'No point in it . . .'

'So you think now!' the doctor interrupted. His voice grew sterner. 'Don't be so stupid, boy. Life is still ahead of you! Life's worth living, even with half a leg gone . . .'

'No!' cried the young soldier, writhing in his bed. 'No!' He died before I was discharged from hospital.

My head hurt and I felt wretched. I couldn't eat, and my temperature was rising rapidly. Since she could not find the

doctor then on duty, the nurse fetched the medical super-
intendent of the hospital himself – a high-up army surgeon.

He examined me, asked a couple of questions, and then
made a brief diagnosis. 'Flu.'

I had to stay in hospital, tossing and turning sleeplessly in
bed, and feeling terribly thirsty. The nurse brought me pills,
different pills every hour – no end of pills, big ones and little
ones, all different colours and sizes. And they all, without
exception, tasted horrible and made me feel even worse. I did
not want to take any more pills, so I put the whole lot –
everything the nurse gave me – into a tin. In a week's time
the tin was nearly full, and I was feeling better.

'Well, it looks as if we can discharge you now!' said the
nurse.

I was so pleased that I made her a present of my tin, pills
and all. She looked first surprised, then annoyed, and marched
out of the room.

'She's off to tell the boss!' surmised my neighbour in the
next bed.

When I went for my discharge papers, the medical super-
intendent gave me a thunderous look. 'You can be thankful
you're on your way out, or I'd have seen you were for it!' he
shouted.

I didn't know what he meant. But he stood up, hands on
the table top. 'What was the idea, eh? Disobeying orders! If I
prescribe pills for you then you take those pills, understand?
If you don't, you're disobeying an order, understand? Why,
I could have you locked up, you – you . . .' He picked my
discharge papers up from his desk and flung them on the floor
at my feet.

The Military Academy

The sergeant-major counted off the doors along the dark corridor, showed us into our room, and then went on to the next room with some of the others.

Our first reaction was one of disappointment as we stood there in the attic room, staring down at the parade ground through the small window, which began at knee level and ended at chest height. There were old, ugly buildings all around.

'I always imagined the military academy a bit grander than this!' someone said, and we all agreed.

Except for one man, who immediately sat down at the table, asked us our names and wrote them down on his notepad. He then asked for the date of every man's promotion to corporal. It turned out that he was the senior man among us. He prepared a room list in elegant lettering, put his own name at the head, as room leader, and hung the whole thing on the door.

Meanwhile, we had begun to unpack our things and put them away in the lockers, but he ordered us to stop.

'Delusions of grandeur, eh?' someone inquired.

'No!' said the man addressed. 'I'm the room leader here, right?' And he rearranged the distribution of beds and lockers.

We let him have his way. We took our things out of the lockers we ourselves had chosen and put them in the ones that he allotted us.

'We are going to be the smartest room in this building!' he said. I found that he had given me the first set of room duties. We were really all so taken aback by his behaviour that we hardly even thought of objecting.

Before he put his clothes away in his own locker, he took a ruler out of his pack, folded each garment to the same thickness, and measured it.

The rest of us watched, fascinated. 'Why on earth are you doing that?' asked the man who had the locker next to mine.

'Because I want to be a German officer!' he replied proudly, straightening his back.

We stood around the big sandbox in the lecture room, while the first lieutenant marked out the position of the fronts with little paper flags stuck in the sand. When he had finished, he explained the situation in the theatre of war represented by this sandbox, and assigned us our various commands. He himself took the part of the enemy. I was supposed to be commanding a platoon stationed on some heights.

The first lieutenant began to make the enemy's moves, penetrating our lines on either side of my heights.

My 'commander-in-chief' pulled our front back, but failed to give me any orders, so that I and my platoon were left on our heights, cut off from the rest with the enemy threatening to cut off our retreat to our own lines.

'So now what do you do?' the first lieutenant asked me.

'I – I order my platoon to fall back towards our own lines until we're in communication with our troops again.'

The lieutenant looked sharply at me. 'Did you have any orders to do that?'

'Er . . . no,' I said. 'But I'm responsible for my men – and it won't do any good for me to sacrifice them in some forlorn hope or get them all taken prisoner! So I shall evacuate the heights!'

'Oh, come, what's the matter with you?' said the first lieutenant. 'How do *you* know what plans Command may have for you and your platoon? Do you know just how much may depend on your holding these heights? Maybe Command intends to counterattack, and they're relying on you to give supporting fire from that position!'

'But suppose the counterattack is beaten off?' I asked.

'Then you and your platoon make an all-round defence!' shouted the lieutenant.

'We haven't got any provisions. And no supplies could reach us. So if we make an all-round defence the wounded will die, without medical aid,' I said. 'And I don't think that could be what Command wants, so that's why I would give orders to withdraw.'

'Now you just listen to me!' The lieutenant was controlling himself with an effort. 'You've no business to be doing your own thinking – you can leave that to Command. Your job is to stick it out where you were stationed. You have to hold your position to the last man!'

All of a sudden the food got worse. We had stew every day – even the stew seemed thinner than before – and it ran out earlier than usual too.

We hoped for our normal Sunday dinner: a thin slice of roast meat, potatoes and red cabbage. But we were disappointed. Sunday brought stew again.

Our timetable was altered as well. Previously, we had been studying a number of different subjects, but now we found ourselves spending hour after hour on the study of various methods of attack.

We went out on field exercises: attack, attack, and more attack. It was a whole week before we discovered the reason for all this. The military academy was to be inspected by a general, and we were being prepared for this occasion. On Tuesday, the entire afternoon was left free so that we could get our uniforms and our quarters spick and span, and in the evening there was a rehearsal for the inspection.

The general turned up on Wednesday. He was quite elderly, and the hand at the peak of his cap trembled as he walked along our front rank, saluting.

We displayed the attacking manœuvres we had learnt on field exercises, and answered all his questions promptly and clearly. The general, well satisfied, beamed at us, gave those officer cadets who had answered the questions a friendly pat on the shoulder, and congratulated our officers in tones audible to everyone. Afterwards he had dinner in our mess, seating himself with us cadets. It was a feast. We had real meat broth, potatoes and peas, plenty of roast meat and gravy, followed by blancmange and even coffee. We had never had a meal such as this before!

During coffee, the general got up and made a speech. He was only sorry, he said, that he couldn't spend longer with us. He was extremely pleased with our excellent standard of achievement, and he wanted to thank the officers training us. Moreover, he added, he must not forget to thank those who were also responsible for creating the conditions in which we worked so well! 'I've seen for myself the way they look after you here,' he finished. 'So my special thanks, and yours too, I am sure, my dear young fellows, to the kitchens!'

It was getting dark by the time I found him. He presented his rifle, ordered me to halt, and then came closer and asked to see my pass. He stood to attention when he saw the braid on my uniform, and at last he recognized me.

'You!' he said quietly, still standing to attention. 'What are you doing here?'

'I got leave for the weekend, so I could come and see you,' I told my father.

'Oh, and I'm on duty Saturday and Sunday – what a shame!' he said.

However, the company commander, an elderly man himself, let my father off duty.

It was both too late and too dangerous to go out. There were Polish resistance fighters around the camp, who attacked German soldiers by night, disarmed them and stripped them of their uniforms. So we sat in my father's room to talk. One by one the other occupants of the room came in, men who, like my father, had already fought in the First World War, and had now joined up again as privates or lance-corporals. They were rather alarmed to see a sergeant sitting in their room.

My father introduced me, but the awkwardness remained; they stayed on their feet, sitting down only when expressly asked to do so, and as soon as I spoke to one of them he would jump up again and salute. My father tried to include them in our conversation, but they just sat round the table like obedient schoolboys, silent except for replies of, 'Yes, sir!' and 'No, sir!'

In the end my father and I went and sat on his bed in the corner to go on with our conversation. One by one the other men, still silent, went off to the washroom, and when they were ready for bed one of them reported to me, in his pyjamas.

The orderly corporal appeared to check the room out. He was a man with a grey moustache, wearing an Iron Cross from the First World War. When no one spoke up to report the room ready for the night, he took a deep breath and was about to begin bawling them out . . . then he saw me sitting in the corner. 'Oh, I beg your pardon, sir!' he said in a whisper. He retreated backwards from the room.

I was eighteen years old.

We were to act as a scout patrol and spy out the terrain.

Six of us covered the area, and we finished up huddled behind a hedge, where we spent the rest of the night. Our stomachs were grumbling.

'Let's go and find some breakfast!' someone suggested in the morning.

The first house we came to belonged to a Polish family. We knocked and marched straight in, dirty as we were, holding our weapons.

The mistress of the house retreated in alarm, backing up against the kitchen wall. We made gestures, trying to convey that we wanted something to eat. Though she still looked scared, the Polish woman drew chairs up to the table for us, and fetched bread – a loaf as long as your arm. She made some coffee, and even produced sugar and honey.

We sat down, our guns between our knees, spread the bread thickly with honey and put plenty of sugar in our coffee. The coarse bread tasted marvellous.

The Polish woman stood by the kitchen stove, watching with frightened eyes as we ate, but whenever we looked directly at her she forced a smile.

When we had finished breakfast, there was still some bread left over, a chunk about the size of a brick.

Our patrol leader asked in sign language if we had to pay, rubbing his thumb and forefinger together. The Polish woman gestured with both hands, dismissing the suggestion, bowed time and time again, and opened the door for us. While her back was turned, one of the men took the end of the loaf off the table and put it in his haversack.

'Why did you pinch that bread?' I asked him, outside.

'We never get bread like that in camp!' he said. 'Besides, these Poles still have far too much!'

A week later we were promoted to the rank of second lieutenant.

Officer

Led by the regimental adjutant, we entered the mess for the first time. A white-jacketed orderly met us, took us to the cloakroom and showed us which pegs were not already commandeered by other officers. 'You're in luck; the Colonel's in a good mood,' he told us in a whisper.

We hung up our belts and caps, combed our hair once again, and straightened our backs. We were ready!

The orderly opened the door of the big dining-room and showed us in. The officers of the regiment were sitting at a horseshoe-shaped table, looking at us.

'Well, so you're our batch of brand-new lieutenants!' said the Colonel, by way of greeting. He raised his monocle to his eye and scrutinized us.

The adjutant introduced us all, reading our names from a list in alphabetical order. Each man bowed when his name was mentioned. Then we went all along the table, introducing ourselves again in person, and learning the names of the other officers present in the process. I ended up sitting on the inside of the horseshoe, right opposite the Colonel.

Dinner began with selected hors d'oeuvres, during which course the Colonel asked me where I came from.

The main course was served, and the Colonel asked about my experience at the front.

Then came dessert, and the Colonel talked about the military academy. He raised his glass to drink my health. I pushed my chair back, jumped to my feet, picked up my own glass and held it in the correct manner, its rim on a level with the third button on my uniform jacket.

'No, no, don't get up!' said the Colonel, when I was already on my feet.

We both sipped from our glasses, returned them to the prescribed level, and looked at one another. An orderly straightened my chair for me, and I sat down again.

When coffee was served, the Colonel began telling stories of the days when he himself was a lieutenant, speaking in such a loud voice that everyone had to listen. And the officers listened attentively, from the lieutenant-colonel down to the youngest lieutenant, while the orderlies moved about on tiptoe.

When he had finished his stories, the Colonel rose. As he did so, he asked me, rather surprisingly, 'Can you play Duffer?' Duffer was a card game.

'No, sir!' I replied.

He regarded me with incredulity. 'You can't play Duffer?' he exclaimed. 'Then how in the world did you ever become an officer?'

The rain was softening up the terrain; it was full of muddy places and dirty puddles, without any good-sized patches of firm, dry ground left anywhere.

However, the morning's exercise had been decided over a week ago: advancing in open country. And the C.O. insisted that we stick to our schedule, come what may.

I went from platoon to platoon and from section to section, supervising the manœuvres. As soon as they saw me approaching, the N.C.O.s ordered the recruits to fling themselves on the ground and crawl through the mud.

At the order 'Take cover!' the men had to drop flat, making the water splash up chest-high. Their uniforms were drenched, and stiff with mud.

There was only one section, belonging to the third platoon,

which still looked clean. They had not yet moved from the starting point. This section consisted entirely of middle-aged men, no doubt fathers of families.

The section leader reported them present, and then turned to them to explain the correct use of the terrain, going into matters like camouflage and the way to dig yourself in.

The men listened, giving intelligent answers.

'This is supposed to be a field exercise, not an instruction period!' I interrupted.

One man raised his hand. 'Sir, we asked the corporal if we couldn't do the manœuvres some other time instead,' he explained. 'Because of the weather.'

'I suppose you think we're fighting this war indoors when it rains?' I said. Turning to the section leader, I told him, 'Go on, get moving!'

'Take cover!' he ordered at once.

The men looked about reluctantly for a clean place to lie down.

'That won't do!' I told them. ' "Take cover" means you've got to get right down, as low as you possibly can.' I stationed myself at the edge of a particularly muddy hollow in the ground, and with all of them looking at me, I lay down flat, pressing myself into the dirt.

One by one the middle-aged men of the section had to follow my example, and I did not move on until they had finished. My uniform was filthy all over – but my batman would put that right.

The three corporals met me in the corridor and reported off duty. 'Better not count on us for any night manœuvres today, sir!'

'Why?'

'We've got a bet on,' explained the youngest. 'We want to

see who can get through a crate of beer and a bottle of brandy fastest! The loser pays two-thirds of the bill, and whoever comes second pays the other third.'

'Any other prizes?' I asked.

'No, it's for the honour of the thing, sir!' the eldest man told me. 'The honour of being the best drinker in the company! That's me at the moment, and I'm going to keep it that way!'

'Well, we'll know by midnight!' the younger N.C.O. interrupted. 'There's a place down in town where we won't be disturbed,' he told me. 'The bottles are already getting cool!'

They all three saluted and set off.

I went into the guardroom, looked at the guardbook, and then lay down on my bed, fully clothed. I hung my steel helmet at the head of the bed, ready to hand. The alarm clock went off at midnight. I put my steel helmet on and went my rounds. When I had inspected the sentries I went to look for the spot in the fence where men without passes used to climb in and out. Here I met the three corporals again.

Swaying on their feet, and babbling to each other, the two older men were approaching me holding the feet of the youngest, and dragging him along behind them. His back and head were bumping along the ground; his uniform and face were soiled, and the entire party stank of beer and vomit.

'Putting him – putting him to bed!' muttered the eldest He slapped his own chest, proudly. 'I'm still the besht – besht drinker!' He looked on the point of collapse. '*Him –*' and he jerked his head backwards – 'he just couldn't take it!' 'He'sh – he'sh only nineteen, anyway!'

The C.O. gave orders for a 'Ladies' Night', for the officers' benefit. The preparations kept an experienced staff sergeant busy for a week. He booked the hotel annexe, had invitations printed and sent to the usual addresses (they were always the same), had decorations put up in the room, got hold of enough drink and ordered fillings for the sandwiches, and finally put on a white jacket to act as waiter at the party.

We had been expecting our guests for almost an hour. The beer was getting warm and the sandwiches were drying up. So far, only four of the ladies invited had turned up. They were sitting in the middle of us young lieutenants, listening to our broad jokes and giggling. They liked this sort of thing, and were perfectly familiar with it. They would go to any party where they were allowed.

A group of older men, first lieutenants, were playing Skat in a corner, while some other officers discussed military matters. A squeaky gramophone was playing popular songs in the background.

The C.O. looked angry; he was drinking hard. As he held out his glass for a refill, he asked the staff sergeant whether the invitations had been properly sent out. The sergeant assured him that the most reliable of the recruits had delivered them.

The C.O. drained his glass again; his eyes were vacant, and he seemed to be brooding. Suddenly he beckoned to me.

I went over, and bent down to hear him, because he was speaking in a low voice. His breath smelled of the red wine he was drinking. 'Got a special mission for you!' he said. 'Since you're the youngest present!' He spoke even more quietly. 'You're to hunt up a partner for every gentleman in this room within the hour. Understand?' He laid a friendly hand on my shoulder. 'And mind they're pretty, young man!' Suddenly he was stern again. 'That's an order!' An amiable smile again, the smile of a superior officer. 'I'm sure you won't disappoint us! Off you go, now, my boy!' He dismissed me.

I buckled on my belt and took my cap off the peg. The

staff sergeant grinned as I went out. 'There's always some of 'em standing around, a couple of streets off, sir,' he whispered to me.

I began approaching girls and women sitting alone before I even left the hotel lounge. But I got most of our guests down by the station.

My own partner was taller than me. I wondered desperately what to talk to her about. We began by exchanging stiff civilities as we cast around in vain for any likely topic of conversation. We tried hard: stilted questions and answers followed one another. It was some time before conversation really began to flow, and when it did we were talking about officers.

She could discuss officers all right; she told me that she really loved listening to officers. She knew quite a number of the kind of stories they told herself. Then she told me about her fiancé, a second lieutenant who had been killed eighteen months ago. She went on in this vein for the rest of the evening, and even on the way home she was still telling stories. There was no need for me to say another word.

We walked side by side through the darkened streets of the town, where there were still a few people about. Once outside the town, she took my arm, and I walked slowly off into the unknown with her. She guided me off the main road, along minor roads and paths through the cornfields. It was a warm night in early summer. The stars were twinkling, and there was a scent of hay. The path became narrower and narrower.

Suddenly a big building loomed up in the dark ahead of us. I saw a farmyard with a tall gate, surrounded by fields and meadows; no lights anywhere.

'This is where I live,' she said. 'They'll all be in bed by now.'

74

We stood face to face, and she put boths hands on my shoulders. Her fingers stroked my lieutenant's stripes. 'Now if you just had a star here,' she murmured, resting her thumbs on the ends of the stripes, 'then I'd kiss you!'

The C.O. handed me my pass. 'Well, this is the first time you go on leave as an officer!' he said. 'Enjoy yourself!'

It was difficult to find a room in the little watering-place, but I got one by applying to the official branch leader of the Party. The very next day all the local girls were queueing up to entertain me during my leave. Their families invited me home to meals, and it became quite difficult to find enough flowers to take with me as presents for my hostesses on my daily visits.

The girls got hold of a bicycle for me, and on Sunday we all rode off to the near-by river, where we sunbathed, swam, ate a picnic and talked. I invented stories about my heroic deeds, and the girls believed every word.

It was quite late when we packed up our things, loaded them on the bicycles, and rode back singing. Our way led through fields, with trees growing at regular intervals along the road. There was no vehicle anywhere in sight, no one at all but us. I put on a spurt, leaving the girls behind. When I was far enough ahead I took my one hand off the handlebars and did some stunt riding, swerving from side to side across the road. I looked back, and saw that the girls were in fits of laughter. Then I took my pistol out of my holster and began firing at the trees along the road. I went on until the magazine was empty. I felt like a real hero!

'Yours is the marching unit from Building 3,' said the C.O. 'You're escorting the men to the West. The train will be ready to take them on board from 10.30 tomorrow. You can

75

have a sergeant and a couple of corporals. They'll report to you after dinner.'

We had the marching unit on parade that afternoon. The two corporals had to go along the corridors of the building five times to hunt everyone out, and after that it was still some time before we got the unit properly drawn up. It numbered more than two hundred soldiers, all tall, broad-shouldered men who moved slowly. Despite their field-grey uniforms, they spoke poor German; the language they spoke among themselves sounded more like Polish.

'Conscripted Germans, this lot!' said the sergeant. 'You know, they could make mincemeat of us if they felt like it.'

Neither the sergeant nor the corporals were willing to travel in the goods trucks along with the men.

Finally we started off, three hours late and without a guard on the train. We issued rations, and otherwise left the men to their own devices.

'We're never going to get this unit to its destination complete!' said the sergeant.

We made quite a long stop at a station along the line where we got coffee. The men stayed in or near the trucks, while we, their escorts, sat at a table with our mugs. Suddenly about ten soldiers came up to us, jabbering something incomprehensible in their own language. Then they seized us, removed our boots and carried them off.

We were so taken by surprise that we did nothing at all. There we sat, in our stocking-feet, staring at each other in horror.

'This'll mean a court martial for us!' groaned the sergeant. 'We should have shot at them! Or shouted for help, anyway!'

'But why didn't they disarm us?' asked one of the corporals. He drew out his pistol. 'Do you think . . . ?'

'No, I don't!' said the sergeant. 'We'd just make ourselves

76

look silly! There are two hundred of them – and four of us. Without any boots either!' He laughed, bitterly.

While we were still wondering what to do, the soldiers reappeared in the doorway with our boots – cleaned and polished! They put them back on us the way they had taken them off, holding us still as they did the job.

'They're not a bad lot after all!' said the sergeant, when the men had gone off again. 'Too good for cannon-fodder, really!'

The train was surely going much too fast.

I sat at the window, facing the way we were going and looking out. Trees, fences, houses all whisked past. At this speed, everything in the compartment rattled.

Suddenly I saw earth spurt up beside the railway embankment. I had never seen anything quite like it before; the spurting seemed to keep pace with the train. As we raced past a signal box I saw plaster flaking from its wall. I was puzzled, and angry with the engine driver for going even faster.

The whole carriage was rattling, and hopping about as if it would leap off the rails.

Not till then did I hear the pounding. The train had a flat wagon at the end, with an anti-aircraft gun on it, and the pounding noise was the firing of this gun. By now my fellow passengers too had realized what was going on outside. Someone jumped up and flung the door open; the others pulled him back. Then we all threw ourselves down in a heap on the dirty floor of the compartment. I knew there was no point in it, but I did the same as the rest, pushing myself in among them.

Somewhere a woman screamed.

At last the train began to slow down, the brakes were applied . . . the door was open! We ran for our lives, down the embankment. Old men, women, children, soldiers, across a marshy meadow, driven on by fear.

I ran with them.

Our flight ended in a spinney; the firing had long since ceased, and we stood there among the trees looking back at the train. The gun was still swivelling on the flat wagon. Steam and water leaked from innumerable hits made on the engine. A dead man hung head down from the window of the driver's cab, and badly wounded people were crawling down the embankment, screaming out loud.

A night field exercise, plus a fifty-kilometre march with full equipment.

The company was deployed, with platoon following platoon at rather long intervals. The soldiers were silent as they carried their packs; their grim, tired faces were covered with stubble. They plodded on, exhausted, dragging their feet along the road.

A corporal carrying several guns brought up the rear, urging the footsore men on.

The C.O. came out on horseback to meet us on the outskirts of the town. He was rested and freshly shaven. He stopped by the roadside to inspect us.

The march past was not a success.

'You're a disgrace! I've never seen anything like it!' he told us. 'If something's not done at once, the unit is marching the whole way back! Now, let's have a song!'

The front section ran through the beginning of the hastily chosen song, and counted, 'Three – four!'

The men straightened their backs and closed ranks in a hurry. '*Oh, the lovely Westerwald . . .* ' they sang. But it was a poor start.

'Singing, halt! Now, let's have a song!'

'*Oh, the lovely Westerwald* . . . ' The soldiers were trying hard, but still it was a poor, thin song.

'Singing, halt! Left turn! Forward march!'

And the entire company began to march back the way it had come.

'Let's have a song!'

'*Oh, the lovely Westerwald* . . . ' Desperately, the soldiers bellowed out their song in praise of the beauties of the Westerwald district.

'Singing halt! Let's have a song!'

'*Oh, the lovely Westerwald* . . . ' The singing was getting worse rather than better.

'Bloody fools!' yelled the C.O. 'You're not even trying! Singing halt! Now, let's have a song!'

'*Oh, the lovely Westerwald* . . . ' The men put everything they had into the song, as tears of rage sprang to their eyes. Their hands clutched at the straps of their rifles, and they kicked the shins of any shirkers remorselessly.

'That's better! Why couldn't you sing it like that to start with?' The C.O. brought his horse to a standstill. 'Singing, halt! Left turn – forward march!'

Immensely relieved, we set off back in the direction of the town again. The C.O. rode at our head on his horse. 'And *now* let's have a song!'

'*Oh, the lovely Westerwald* . . . '

'And again! In case you forget it!'

'*Oh, the lovely Westerwald* . . . '

We were still singing '*Oh, the lovely Westerwald*' as we marched into the barrack square.

The notes of the last waltz died away, the girls from the Bund Deutscher Mädel were sent home, and the farewell party was over.

The leader of the Women's League, who had provided the cakes, and the leader of the girls who had been celebrating at the party with the soldiers, were each given two bottles of the wine that was left over, and then they left too. Out in the street I thanked them once again for their help, and we said goodbye.

It was a warm night; there was no moon. As I went back into the hall, the last couples were leaving by the back door. My sergeant and a private were waiting in the next room. We did up our belts, put our steel helmets on and made sure our torches were working.

'I hate this job,' grumbled the sergeant.

We started out. The dance hall backed on to a park which had two gates. We moved off towards the gate behind the hall, going the shortest way and making a lot of noise. As soon as they saw us, several couples hurried away from the benches and left the park.

'Three hours ago they hadn't even met!' said the sergeant, crossly.

We locked the gate, and then slowly combed through the park towards the other gate, searching it bush by bush, shining our torches into every group of trees.

We found one couple behind a bush; she was forty, the soldier was about eighteen. The sergeant found a piece of paper among the woman's documents and unfolded it. 'Who's that?' he asked.

'My husband!' she said pertly.

'Killed two months ago!' commented the sergeant, folding up the notification of death again. 'You make me want to spit!' he said, as he returned her papers to her. And he did spit.

In the West

We were on our way to the front. Whenever the train slowed down, the soldiers would jump out of the goods trucks on to the embankment and run alongside it. I reminded them at every stop that they were to leave the trucks only by my express order, or during an air raid, but it was no good. The men were sick and tired of staying in the trucks while we made such slow progress.

I set a double guard on the train, but the men on duty refused to discipline their companions. 'We're not recruits now!' they said. No sooner did we slacken speed a little than they were all standing on the running boards again, ready to jump off.

The C.O. reprimanded me, and I lost my temper with the men. I bawled at them, shouted, threatened . . .

None of it did any good.

Next time we made a fairly long halt, near a large town, I lined them all up in heavy marching order. Standing on the loading platform, I went over the regulations for their benefit once again, finishing, 'My patience is exhausted!'

Some of them smiled at this – a small lieutenant, nineteen years old, preaching them such a sermon!

I marched them from the platform to a football ground which I had seen from the station. People in the surrounding houses opened their windows, and a number of spectators gathered on the playing field. Out there, in front of everyone, I made the men do rifle drill, run, bend knees, crawl . . . for over an hour.

Sweating and dirty, they marched back to the cramped goods trucks, where there was no water.

As we started off again I made them sing a song which ran, '*It's a fine life in the Army . . .* '

The engine pulled our trucks into a siding, and then went off.

'You've got at least an hour's wait,' a railwayman told us.

Instantly, soldiers came flocking out of all the open hatches, stretched, brushed the straws off their uniforms, and went in search of water.

However, the large French railway station had suffered badly from bombing raids. Posts had fallen across the tracks, overhead leads hung down to the sleepers, and there was no water anywhere.

'You'll have to go into town,' said the railwayman.

A private from the truck we were using as a kitchen put on his cap, did up his belt, and left the station in search of drinking water, carrying two buckets. As he went, he waved a cheerful good-bye to the corporal acting as company cook. 'What d'you bet there's something doing here?'

The rest of us waited. And waited. An hour later, the private was still not back.

'I reckon I know where he is!' said the cook.

We picked a search party to go and look for the man and his two buckets. 'Try that way,' the railwayman advised us. 'That's where they mostly go first.' He pointed.

A long line of German soldiers was standing in front of a house in a narrow street, close to the famous cathedral. At regular intervals the door opened, and a medical corps sergeant would let one soldier out and another in. Those leaving grinned broadly at the men in the queue, pointing back at the house with unmistakable gestures of satisfaction as they put away their paybooks in their breast pockets. All the house windows were thickly curtained, but now and then a curtain in one of the windows would be pushed aside a little way, and a woman's face looked down at the long queue of waiting soldiers.

Our private was standing in the queue, not far from the door. Both his buckets were full. 'Well, how was I to know it would take so long?' he said, by way of explanation.

The straight road stretched endlessly ahead. There was not a breath of wind to stir the poplars, and the sun was softening the tarmac. Grumbling, the soldiers dragged their packs on towards the front, making very slow progress. They stopped in every patch of shade, groaning, drank, wiped the sweat away, and demanded a rest.

Two men in particular seemed to be complaining all the time. Both of them had only recently been let out of the cells and put into our marching unit. They stirred up the others.

When we stopped in a village for yet another rest, a staff sergeant brought the pair of them across to me. They saluted sloppily and stared around them as they stood before me.

'I doubt if there are any motor vehicles available round here,' I said. 'But suppose we had a horse and cart, we could use it to carry our packs.'

'Yes, sir,' they muttered, but they were beginning to take a bit more notice.

'And we could march more easily without our packs, couldn't we?'

The two men exchanged glances, and grinned. This time their 'Yes, sir!' was a lot brighter.

'Any idea how we could get hold of one? Maybe you'll think of something. We start off again in an hour's time.'

'Yes, sir!' said both, in chorus, and they turned and went. As they walked off I saw one dig the other in the ribs.

Half an hour later a large, flat-bottomed cart trundled into the square where we were resting. It was big enough to take all the packs, as well as those men who were badly footsore.

The cart was pulled by two big, sleek, well-rested horses. They pawed the ground impatiently as we stowed our things in the cart. I examined the harness and the cart itself, but there was no indication of the owner's name. 'Er – where did you get this cart?'

'Found it, sir!' both men said smartly.

I asked no more questions.

It was appallingly hot. We sheltered from low-flying planes and from the sun under trees and bushes, where we lay sweating, stripped to the waist.

When the C.O. summoned us I simply dragged my uniform shirt over my head as I went off to find him.

We came up from four different directions: a first lieutenant with only one eye and three second lieutenants, one of them dragging a foot, another with a mutilated hand, and the third was me. All of us in shirt-sleeves.

The C.O. was waiting for us in the middle of the yard, in full uniform, legs straddled. He began shouting at us even before we reached him. As officers, he yelled, we had to preserve our dignity in *all* circumstances! Why, our shirts didn't even indicate rank!

'Yes, sir!' said the first lieutenant, turning to go back.

However, the C.O. stopped him. 'Yes, well, stay as you are for the moment, gentlemen,' he said, more mildly. 'I have something important to discuss with you.'

We stood to attention in front of him, in the blazing sun, exposed to any low-flying aircraft.

'Heroic speech coming up!' whispered the lieutenant beside me.

84

The C.O. strode up and down in front of us in silence, gazing at the ground and rubbing his nose with his right forefinger. After pacing up and down three times he suddenly stopped. 'Gentlemen!' he began.

We jumped, and looked at him.

'Gentlemen! Our job is to take reinforcements to the front. Well, you know your men. It's not the very best of material we're taking to relieve our brave comrades at the front: convalescents, men with no combat experience, jailbirds, draft dodgers. However, gentlemen, you also know that your example, your own personal example, can inspire even this basically poor human material!' He interrupted himself to point at our shirts, remarking, 'And that goes for your appearance too!'

We exchanged glances. But the C.O. was going on with his speech.

'Your duty, gentlemen, is to live and die setting an example to these men!' He paused, significantly. 'Gentlemen, I expect that some of you will come out of this action with high – with the very highest – distinction. Nor will we shrink from sacrifice . . . ' And he interrupted himself again in mid-speech. 'But first things first! You will now immediately hold a finger-nail inspection . . . '

Up in the sky, a swarm of enemy fighters was assembling.

The unit had withdrawn to fill in a bombed embankment. I was left behind with a few men.

The sun was blazing, though it was still morning. The soldiers crawled into the cool shade of the barn, and I took my blanket a little further off and spread it out in the middle of a large, empty meadow. There was not a soul anywhere in sight. I put my uniform and underclothes in a pile beside the blanket and lay naked in the sun. Then I fell asleep.

I heard the sound of an engine. Three twin-fuselage fighters, flying over the meadow.

I wanted to shut my eyes again. They turned and circled above the meadow, describing a wide arc. I looked up at them, almost surprised as the first came in to attack.

To attack *me*! I jumped up and raced over the meadow.

The rattle of the aircraft gun drowned out the sound of the engine. Then it stopped and I heard the engine roar again as the shadow of the plane chased over me. As it flew off, the rattle of the aircraft gun came again.

I ran on across the meadow. The second plane was coming up already, flying even lower. Shots tore into the ground.

I reached the stream and threw myself in; I cowered on the narrow stream-bed, digging myself into the gravel, held my breath and put my face in the water . . .

There were no more shots, only the hum of the engines flying away.

The people of the town had either left, or were in their cellars waiting for us to go away. Our unit was the only one occupying the place. We lounged around in the small park, drinking wine – excellent wine found in the near-by houses.

There was a shot, and an old Frenchwoman came running towards us screeching and waving her arms, and talking so fast and in such agitation that no one could understand a word she said. She kept pointing in the same direction.

Another shot.

We picked up our guns, and four of us went off to the building indicated by the old lady. She refused to go with us.

A third shot.

Taking off our safety catches, we entered the house, to be met by the hollow report of yet another shot.

As we went along the passages inside the house, we tried to locate the gunman; we thought he was in the last room but one on the first floor. We heard the click of his weapon, and the fifth shot echoed through the house.

Before the marksman had a chance to fire another shot, the corporal kicked the door in and jumped aside. We all pointed our guns at the doorway.

'Hands up! Come on out of there!'

A lance-corporal from our own unit appeared in the doorway, still holding his rifle. He gazed stupidly at us.

'What are you shooting at?'

He took us into the room and showed us a large safe. 'There could still be some money in there!' he insisted. 'I was trying to shoot the lock off!'

The staff sergeant took his gun away from him. 'You know the penalties for looting?' he inquired.

There were four big, man-sized casks in the cellar. Three of them had both ends knocked out, but the fourth still held cider. We filled our mugs and drank, and decided to spend the night here; the cellar seemed to be solidly built, and the sounds of fighting outside hardly penetrated to us.

'I'm going to sleep in this cask,' said the company leader. 'It'll keep falling plaster off my head.'

We ate some rolls, drank cider, and had some chocolate taken from a burnt-out chocolate factory. Then we padded the casks with straw and crawled in. Our voices sounded so funny and hollow inside the casks that we even observed the courtesies and said, 'Good night!' The wood smelled of alcohol, and made us drowsy.

I woke up when the last dispatch rider came back from taking a message. He stared at us in our casks, roared with laughter, and finally asked the company leader if there was another cask for him. Sleepily, the company leader told him, 'Get one yourself!'

All was quiet again in the cellar.

I heard the dispatch rider fill first his field flask and then a bucket with cider. Suddenly there was a loud crash. We shot out of our casks in alarm, to find a river of cider flowing over our feet. The dispatch rider had knocked out the bottom of the half-full cask. When it was empty, he wiped it dry with some straw and lay down to sleep.

A hundred or so litres of cider trickled away over the cellar floor.

'You could come, sir,' suggested the corporal. 'You can command the tank.'

'I've never been in a tank, though. I don't know anything about it.'

'Oh, that's all right,' said the corporal. 'Hop in, sir. Time we got started, or we'll never get out of here.'

I clambered up into the tank turret.

The corporal had a map; he showed me the only streets that still led out of the pocket where we were now. He also told me the more important phrases of command.

In the evening twilight, we rolled out of a French farmyard with two other tanks in our wake. We got as far as the all-important main road. It was quite a narrow road, with dense thickets on the left-hand side. There were vehicles waiting there, stretching as far as the eye could see: lorries, horse-drawn carts, jeeps, buses. Troops marched along among them. A few motorcycles managed to ride along the side of the endless queue, but the queue itself was moving forward at snail's pace.

I gave the order to halt.

'What's up?' asked the corporal, down below.

'The road's jammed full. We'll have to wait and filter into the stream of traffic.'

'Filter in!' said the corporal, with some irony, wriggling up to look through the turret hatch. Ahead of us, the columns of men and vehicles were wedged solid.

He shook his head. 'Try filtering into that lot and we'll never get anywhere!' He turned to the driver of the nearest horse-drawn cart. 'Make way!' he shouted.

The driver tapped his forehead. 'Can't!' he shouted back. 'I'm right on the edge of the ditch, can't you see?'

'I don't mind where you are!' said the corporal, through his teeth. Then he bellowed loud enough to be heard right out in the main road. 'Tank advance!'

Slowly, the armoured monster thrust its way forward towards the cart. The horses shied nervously.

The driver swore and lashed out at us with his whip. Finally, however, he had to guide his horses into the ditch, where the cart tilted, and then tipped right over.

'That's the way!' grunted the corporal, pleased. He sent me down below, and I stayed there for the rest of the journey. My head was throbbing with the unaccustomed noise. I was tossed backwards and forwards, and I kept bumping into things.

The corporal himself bulldozed his way through all bottle-necks and over every obstacle. His shouts and curses were audible even above the roar of the tank's engine.

We did not have to stop again. And we got safely out of the pocket . . .

At midday we found the village inn, and went inside. A woman in a dark dress greeted us with a slight inclination of her head, and pointed in silence to the dining-room.

We gaped.

It was a room with a low ceiling of dark brown beams,

almost black, with old engravings on the walls, white table-cloths, vases of flowers everywhere, spotless plates, crystal-clear glasses, silver cutlery, and genuine large napkins.

The few French guests lowered their knives and forks, and their conversation died away. They watched us, their faces hostile.

We hesitated, but then found a table near the door, looked at the menu and chose hors d'oeuvres, fish, meat, vegetables, cheese and wine.

However, before the meal was served I turned to find the woman standing beside my chair with a folded towel over her right arm, like a waiter with a cloth. She cleared her throat quietly.

We broke off our conversation and looked at her, but she said nothing. Since I did not understand what she wanted, I stood up. She put her arm through mine, and with a slight pressure of her hand guided me out of the dining-room, past the kitchen, to a large sink standing out in the yard.

I understood now. I turned on the tap . . .

But she herself pushed back the sleeves of my battledress blouse and my shirt, picked up the soap, washed my hand for me without a word, and dried it with the clean towel, as if it were the most natural thing in the world.

I apologized, and thanked her, and apologized again. She shook her head, refusing my thanks, and guided me back to our table the same way as she had led me out.

The lorry stopped in the market square of the little French town during the night. We got our packs out, jumped down, and the lorry drove on.

We stretched, and looked around. The town was asleep. All the windows round the square were darkened, with not even a streak of light to show that anyone was still awake.

'I know this place!' said the major. 'I'll see about finding us quarters.' He picked up his things and disappeared.

The women intelligence aides put their luggage all together in a heap and sat on it, leaning against one another and yawning. One by one, they fell asleep, still sitting even in their sleep.

I kept myself awake with difficulty, seated on my rucksack, and keeping my open pistol holster thrust forward.

A church clock struck every quarter of an hour. Time passed, and still the major did not come back. I stood up and walked round the sleeping girls in circles, to keep awake.

After an hour had gone by I woke them and told them I was going in search of the major. Before I left, they opened their cases and took out their pistols. Each with a pistol in her lap, they settled down to sleep again.

I went cautiously out of the market place, keeping close to the walls, and into the main street. I had hardly gone a hundred metres before I came upon a dimly lit sign saying *Officers' Hostel*. I rang.

After I had rung three times a sergeant appeared, yawning, and wearing his battledress blouse on top of his pyjama jacket. I inquired about the major.

'Oh, yes, he's here,' said the sergeant drowsily. He took me to the major's room and knocked at the door. It was some time before the major opened it, just a crack. 'What's the idea?' he snapped when he saw me. 'Waking me up in the middle of the night like this!'

'The rest of us are still waiting down in the square!' I told him.

'Well, there was only this one room left,' he said. 'Ask the sergeant if you like!' He added generously, 'I'm sure you'll find somewhere else for yourself and the girls!' and shut the door.

It was quite late when I arrived in the little watering-place. I took two bars of French chocolate out of my pack, and with these in my hand went into the nearest shop, bought some small thing, and asked the girl assistant to gift-wrap the two bars of chocolate for me. Her eyes fastened hungrily on the chocolate, but she even found me a coloured ribbon and did up the little parcel with a big bow.

My present in my hand, my rucksack on my back, I set off for the house.

It was getting dark by now, and I saw an Army car outside the house. I climbed the steps and rang. Silence inside, a long silence, and then footsteps.

They were hers. I recognized all the sounds of the place again.

She had stopped by the mirror in the hall. She'd be passing a comb quickly through her hair.

The door opened.

'You!' she said in surprise.

I held out the parcel of chocolate to her, so that I could have my hand free.

She did not thank me; she seemed to be stuck for words. She remained there in the doorway, the handle in one hand, my chocolate in the other.

I took a step towards her.

'No!' she said. 'I can't let you in. My parents are out.'

I saw an officer's cap and leather belt hanging on a peg.

She noticed my glance. 'It's wartime,' she said. 'How was anyone to know if you'd be coming back again?'

Denmark

Sunday morning in Denmark.

We were waiting for dinner, out of doors, some of us playing table tennis while the others watched. The sun shone in the clear blue sky, and there was a light breeze off the sea.

'Nice weather for an outing!' cried the captain, pointing upwards with his bat.

A gentle humming filled the air, growing louder. Bombers were approaching from the landward side, flying very high, in orderly formations.

'Been unloading their filthy bombs on us back at home again!' snorted the captain.

Suddenly a howling noise, accompanied by a staccato pounding, rose above the hum of the engines.

'Look! Look!' shouted someone, pointing north.

The fighters escorting the bomber formations were flying low, evidently attacking some target on the ground.

'There's nothing of ours that way!' said the captain, taken aback. He threw down his ping-pong bat on the table. 'We'd better get over there, fast.' He was running for the car. 'Here, you know something about low-flying aircraft – you'd better come, will you?' he asked me.

I crouched on the running board, watching the sky as the car drove north along the road. The bomber formations disappeared into the distance, and there was no more sign of the low-flying fighters.

However, there was black smoke rising ahead of us. We drove in that direction, but the road was going to by-pass the source of the smoke. The captain swerved aside into the fields, and we drove across a meadow behind an embankment. The railway tracks ran through this meadow, and a train was standing there, with thick grey smoke rising from the engine.

We stopped, and went closer.

The corpses were lying by the tracks in the meadow, about twenty of them, men, women and children.

We walked down the line.

'Danes, all of them. What had they got to do with the war?' muttered the captain. He saluted the dead and turned away. 'Just going for a Sunday outing!'

My room in the attic had been requisitioned for the German Wehrmacht. It was in a veterinary surgeon's house on the outskirts of the town. I got the key, and moved in.

It was a big room, light and very clean, though sparsely furnished. The way up to it went right through the house and past the family's own rooms. But I never succeeded in introducing myself to the other occupants. As soon as I opened my door, they immediately closed every other door in the place, and when I knocked no one seemed to hear.

Just once, the door of the children's playroom was left open a crack, and a face peered out. But when I looked that way the face disappeared, and the crack was quickly closed. I would go on duty in the morning and come back in the evening, and each time I walked through what might have been an empty house.

This went on for weeks. On Sundays I would sometimes stand at the window and look down into the garden – but no one went out in the garden at this time of year. I spent these autumn evenings sitting in my room reading.

The rooms to the left and right of mine were occupied by maidservants, who sometimes had their boyfriends in. I would hear them creep upstairs in stocking-feet. I heard whispering in the house, and orders being given, kind words and angry ones, crying and laughter – but I never saw anyone at all.

One day, when I was out in town, a sergeant pointed out my host, the vet, to me. I didn't even know what he looked like.

On Martinmas Eve there was a party in the house. Guests had been invited, and I heard the clattering of china in the kitchen, the sound of people talking, someone playing the piano. There was singing.

Late that evening there came a gentle knock on my door, and I called out, 'Come in!' But no one came.

I went to the door and opened it.

On the floor outside stood a big tray, laden with glasses of spirits, wine and beer, all ranged in rows, several pieces of different kinds of cake, some cigarettes, and in the middle, brown and tempting, a leg of the Martinmas goose.

One morning I happened to be complaining about my batman to the sergeant-major. The batman was still a young man, but he was work-shy; he dodged everything he could, and never kept my things really neat and clean. He had his own ways of getting back at me if I called him to order.

'We'll soon put that right, sir!' said the sergeant-major, writing something down in his big notebook. And when I came off duty I noticed that the hinges of my door did not squeal any more; someone must have oiled them.

I went into my room, and stared in surprise.

Everything was in place. The bed was neatly made, the window panes spotless. The floor shone. A small vase of wild flowers stood on the table. My uniform, well brushed, hung in the wardrobe with a pair of gleaming boots below it.

95

The only thing missing was the new batman himself.

I went in search of the sergeant-major, and found him in the N.C.O.s' mess, having a meal. Not wanting to get his greasy fingers on his trousers, he held his arm stiffly downwards as he stood to attention. 'Anything wrong, sir?' he asked apprehensively, with his mouth half full.

'No, everything's fine – but where *is* the man?'

The sergeant-major swallowed his mouthful and chuckled. 'Having a spot of extra drill!' He jerked a thumb downwards. 'He can clean things right enough, but he's no good at anything else!' The sergeant-major grinned at me. 'I'll send him over to you as soon as he gets back, sir.'

That evening the new batman reported to me, still breathing hard. The rim of his uniform cap was damp with sweat, and his battledress blouse flapped around his chest. He could hardly keep upright.

'Would you like to carry on as my batman?'

'Yes, sir!' He suddenly smiled. 'I do all this at home, you know!' He gestured at the room as he spoke. Going over to the wardrobe, he opened the door. 'I saw you still had some dirty washing in here, sir. I'll deal with that right away.' He took the things out of the bottom drawer; still with his arms full of them, he sat down on my bed, uninvited. 'We're a big family at home, you see, sir, and you learn that kind of thing in a big family. Eight children I've got. My eldest, he's twenty now, sir.' I was nineteen years old at the time.

An hour before reveille, the orderly corporal chased them all out of bed, out of their rooms, and into the corridor. They had to parade in night-shirts, still drowsy. Freezing cold, their hair ruffled and their eyelids stuck up, the skinny seventeen and eighteen-year-olds pushed and jostled each other till they found their places. 'What's up?' they asked in whispers.

The orderly corporal did not reply, just marched them to the end of the corridor and reported to the staff doctor.

The doctor put on his white overall and addressed the boys. 'Now then, let's see whether any of you lot have picked up a little present from the girls!' He sat down on a stool, signalling to his two orderlies.

'Is it all right for me to go now?' I asked.

He shook his head. 'Sorry, the rulebook says an officer of the unit must be present.'

I leaned against a window.

'Right, listen!' shouted the sergeant from the medical corps. 'You come up to the doctor here in turn, and do just as you're told. Right then, first ten: shirts raise!'

Reluctantly and much embarrassed, the recruits raised their night-shirts.

'First!'

'Closer!' said the doctor. He told everyone, 'When your turn comes, you pull your shirt up with your left hand and hold your penis in your right!'

The first lad did as the doctor told him. 'Foreskin back – squeeze – foreskin forward – cough – off you go!'

'Next!' called the sergeant.

'Next! . . . Next! . . . Next!'

Bombers returning from raids often flew over our camp. Planes that had been winged were generally flying low as they made their way out to sea, and the barracks would quiver to the roar of the engines. Panes jingled in the window frames and quite often broke.

We used to hide our heads under the blankets.

One night one of these damaged aircraft came down on a dune not far from the barracks and broke up as it crashed. Some bits of it landed on our parade ground. After this, orders were issued for low-flying bombers to be attacked with all available weapons, since their own fighting strength should be considerably reduced.

All the weapons we had were pistols, rifles and machine guns, so we stationed a sentry, with a machine gun mounted on a tripod, on the camp site, fitted the gun with a sight for flying targets, and loaded it with tracer ammunition. Thus equipped, we waited for the next bomber to fly over.

The very next night a straggling formation of three or four aircraft approached, flying low. The man stationed by the machine gun let the bombers come into his sights and then opened fire.

The machine gun spat out at most ten bright green shots in the direction of its target. Then all hell seemed to break loose. The bomber we had attacked instantly returned our fire. A hail of machine gun and aircraft gun fire rained down on the camp as the plane's engines roared. Its companions came to its aid, and one of them even dropped a small bomb.

Our machine gun fell silent, and we all took cover on the ground or under our beds. Next day the order to fire on bombers returning from raids was countermanded.

My grandfather's little house was in ruins. My mother and my grandparents had been evacuated to an area where there were fewer air raids.

I went in search of the house where my mother was living. I walked along grey, monotonous streets. She had a tiny room, crammed with old furniture, on the ground floor of an ugly little terrace house. When I came in she was leaning against a dark-brown kitchen dresser. She stared at me, pale and silent, not even responding to the pressure of my hand.

I put my case down. As she still said nothing, I switched on the radio I saw standing on the dresser.

'Oh, no, don't!' said my mother, taking the plug out of the socket. 'The landlord doesn't allow it – because of the electricity.'

I had to push the table aside before I could sit down. The noise it made caused my mother to jump; she picked the table up and lifted it bodily to move it.

'I haven't heard from Father for ages,' I said, trying to get a conversation going. 'Are the posts any more regular here?'

At this my mother burst into tears, crying quietly but without restraint. She took a dirty, crumpled letter from the dresser and handed it to me. 'I didn't know how to write and tell you,' she whispered incoherently.

My father was reported missing.

Later that evening, Mother made me a sandwich.

I said, 'But Grandfather and Grandmother live in this street too, don't they? Aren't they coming over?'

Mother began to cry again. 'They can't. The landlord won't allow Grandfather in.' And after a long pause she added, timidly, 'You can't stay here either – the landlord won't allow it. He'll give me no peace if you do!' She began to weep out loud for the first time. 'We're only here on sufferance!'

In the East

The soldiers lay on their bunks below decks, reading, sleeping, playing cards or writing home yet again. Five of us officers had been given a roomy cabin. We were all lieutenants, but there was one of us who seemed a lot older that the rest. He also had a distinctive stripe on his sleeve. He belonged to a very well-known unit, made up of specially selected personnel.

It took us some time to introduce ourselves all round, and when we had done so we sat down to our first meal together round the table, which was screwed to the floor. It was laid with several packets of butter, a big pile of bread, some rings of sausage and several lengths of hard salami. We had been issued with a generous quantity of rations for our short voyage.

We were just about to begin our meal when the lieutenant from the special unit drew all the food towards him. We looked at him in surprise.

'What are you doing?' someone asked.

'Going to share it out fairly!' said the officer from the special unit.

'But there's no need!' the rest of us assured him. 'We've got so much we couldn't eat it all anyway.'

'All the same, I intend to share it out!' the older lieutenant insisted.

'But then we shall have to open everything and cut into it,' we objected. 'And the stuff that's left over will dry up, or go bad!'

'Anyway, there isn't space for everyone to keep his own rations separate,' someone remarked.

'And how are we going to pack up all the leftovers when we leave ship?' another man inquired.

The lieutenant went red in the face; his voice was sharp. 'If you really want to know, I think it beneath the dignity of a German officer to start tucking in before we know how much is each man's by right!' He divided everything very meticulously, and sat down on the edge of his bunk, so as not to eat at the same table with us.

I was to report to the divisional commander's adjutant at sixteen hours precisely. I arrived at the command post a quarter of an hour early, and walked up and down between the bunkers to fill in time. Finally I knocked at the adjutant's door on the dot.

'Come in!' he called at once. He looked far from pleased. 'I've been sitting here ten minutes waiting for you. I like to have punctuality!'

I showed him my watch, with the hands only just past four o'clock.

He roared with laughter. 'Call that a watch? No wonder you're late. That's not a watch, that's a child's toy!'

'It was a present from my father,' I replied. 'Anyway, it's the only watch I have.'

He got up, shaking his head, and went over to the corner of the bunker room, where he opened a case. I was left standing by his table.

The adjutant took five or six pieces of white cardboard out of his case, the kind you see displaying merchandise in watch-makers' shops. He put them on the table. Each had several wristwatches strapped to it.

I stared at this display of watches in some surprise.

'We had to clear out a watchmaker's place when we with-drew,' the staff officer explained, 'otherwise the enemy would have got the lot.' He pushed the watches towards me. 'Go on, pick yourself one.' As I made no move, he took off the rubber bands holding a large, square watch to the cardboard, removed my own watch and handed it to me, and strapped on the new one. 'And don't let me find you arriving late in future!' he said, taking the rest of the watches back to the case and lifting the lid. 'Well then, to work!'

I could not help seeing that, besides the watches, his case contained some gold jewellery.

In the afternoon I located the battalion staff of my new unit. They were billeted in a railway station. What had once been the station-master's house was the officers' quarters. The twin beds in the former conjugal bedroom had been placed end to end. I was allotted the bed facing the window; the other one belonged to the paymaster. After I had been shown my quarters, the C.O. showed me round, beginning with the kitchen.

The cook had moved into the left luggage office. He introduced me to his staff, one by one, finishing with a big, strong Russian woman, and then he offered me a snack by way of welcoming me. 'That Russian girl's been with the unit six months now,' said the C.O. grinning, as we left the kitchen. 'She sticks to the kitchen staff – belongs to all of them in common.'

We went over to the signal box, where the telephonists had set up their equipment. The ticket office was occupied by the fat paymaster. He greeted me with a glass of French brandy, and as I left he pressed a large tin of cigarettes into my hand. 'To our future association!' he whispered, winking.

The C.O. had another bottle of brandy himself. He sat down in the station-master's living-room, poured brandy, and told me my duties. The bottle and our conversation were both finished soon after midnight, and I went in search of the conjugal bedroom and my bed. I climbed over men sleeping on the floor all along the corridors and in the rooms I passed through, and I had to push the last one aside, because he was lying right in front of my bedroom door, snoring.

The paymaster was already asleep. I quickly undressed in the dark and crept under the blankets. In my bed I found a pocket flask of cognac. It was not long before I too was asleep.

I woke towards morning, hearing a noise. It was getting light already. The bedroom door opened, slowly and quietly, and the Russian girl, the kitchenmaid, came in on tiptoe. She got into the paymaster's bed as if it were a matter of course.

The paymaster grunted happily.

Our motorbike was up to its hubs in the mud of the ditch. We shovelled and pushed and cursed, but the motorbike and sidecar were too heavy for us; they stuck fast.

Eventually a brand new tractor, its paint bright and shiny, drove up. The driver politely declined to dirty his hands with what he called 'your old rattletrap', and sat in his driving seat while we fastened a cable between the tractor and our bike.

The tractor began to pull. The back end of our motorbike rose slightly, and then the whole machine was hoisted out of the mud and back on the road, with a squelch. The tractor driver undid our cable and drove off.

We scraped the mud off our machine. It took us a long time to get it going again.

As we approached the little town we were stopped by a military policeman. 'The crossing's under fire,' he warned us.

Just then there was a rushing sound overhead; the air pressure generated by the impact raised our sidecar from the ground. 'Heavy shells!' growled the motorbike rider.

We waited for two more bursts of firing. They were coming

at regular intervals, and the shells were being aimed quite accurately at the crossing.

'Well, there's nothing for it!' said the rider. 'We'll have to get over somehow.'

When the second burst of firing was over, he stepped on the gas and let the engine race. The sidecar vibrated.

We listened.

Another burst of firing. Now!

The motorbike jerked and shot forward. We ducked down, swerving wildly to avoid the craters and debris as we made for the crossing. The sidecar seemed to be flying through the air.

As we tore across the road, I saw the tractor lying right across the junction, a wreck of twisted metal. In the middle of the crossing lay the tractor driver, dead. His hands were still clutching his steering wheel.

He was posted to our unit one day: a young lieutenant with a crippled leg. He used a crutch, and obviously walked only with difficulty. The C.O. gave him some kind of clerical work to do.

A week later the new arrival turned up at the C.O.'s office and produced his paybook.

The paybook contained a record of twenty-five days of close combat – exactly twenty-five. Twenty-five times our crippled lieutenant had seen the whites of the enemy's eyes; twenty-five times he and his crutch had faced men throwing hand grenades, soldiers with fixed bayonets, sharpshooters with pistols. He had led counter-attacks – with his crutch. The entries bore an official stamp.

However, the unit which had stamped his book was unable to give us any information, since it no longer existed. It had been wiped out. All material witnesses would be either dead or missing.

The C.O. made a few inquiries of other officers and other commanders and then shrugged his shoulders.

When our new arrival was summoned to Divisional Command, I accompanied him. The walk through trackless country was hard going for him, and he often had to stop, leaning on his crutch and groaning. When some artillery fire came close to us he did not fling himself down, but bent, stiffly. It took him a very long time to walk a short distance, and when we finally got there he was panting and exhausted. He leaned against one of the bunkers and wiped the sweat from his forehead.

We had a short wait, and then I watched the General pin the close combat bar and the Iron Cross, First Class, on the crippled young lieutenant.

The sound of an explosion woke us in the middle of the night. Half dressed, we ran out into the open, ready to fling ourselves to the ground at the next noise we heard.

But all was quiet; there was only the faint sound of fighting at the front, far away. No bombs or firing; nothing.

Part of one hut was destroyed, however. The end of the hut where the least popular of the staff sergeants slept, a man who was generally disliked. We got him out from the debris, dead. And we found another corpse in his bed with him, the body of a girl – a Russian girl who had been with the unit for some months, and was in great demand because of her striking beauty. She was always causing trouble among the N.C.O.s. Now she lay dead beside the sergeant.

Gradually almost all the N.C.O.s assembled by the pile of debris. Without exception, they were correctly dressed. They stood looking at the two corpses, and somehow there was a general feeling of satisfaction.

'Sir,' said a dispatch rider to me, quietly, 'have a look at that hut, will you? That shell didn't come from on top – it came from the side, quite low down. Behind the hut at that!'

'So what?' interrupted a sergeant standing close by, who had overheard. 'Must have been an armour piercing projectile aimed at some tank, gone astray!'

'But then it would have had to pass right through the main building to hit the hut just here! And the main building's made of stone,' the dispatch rider pointed out.

The sergeant turned back to his viewing of the corpses, and said no more.

Suddenly all the N.C.O.s, as one man, began pulling down the remains of the hut. 'In case of fire,' they explained. They worked on their own; they let the men watch, but not help them, and they cleared the ground so thoroughly that there was hardly a trace left of the ruined end of the hut.

The C.O. went to the telephone switchboard. 'Any reports of tanks breaking through this evening?' he asked.

The man at the switchboard shook his head.

'Well, go on, man, find out!' ordered the C.O.

The telephonist plugged things in, wound things up, gave his code, made his inquiry and again shook his head. 'No tanks reported.'

'Funny . . .' murmured the C.O. softly, with a query in his eyes as he looked across at me. Next morning he wrote the staff sergeant's wife a letter in his own hand, telling her that her husband had 'fallen for Germany'.

The local Commissioner for Repatriation had handed over half his house to us. He and his family occupied the top floor, while we took over the dining-room, sitting-room, library, kitchen and part of the cellar.

After about a week, the house came into the line of enemy

fire. The Commissioner closed his files, entrusted his house to us, and left.

No sooner had he gone than we invaded the rooms on the top floor, flinging open cupboard doors, searching for clean underwear, taking shirts and bedclothes.

A sergeant, rummaging in the wardrobe among dress suits, winter coats and brown uniforms, found a leather jacket. A black leather jacket, very useful in cold wet weather. He tried it on, and when he found that it fitted he refused to take it off again.

In the bedroom belonging to the mistress of the house, I found and commandeered a bottle of eau de cologne. I investigated that wardrobe too, and in among the summer dresses and ski pants I found another leather jacket. This one was fawn, almost yellow, had darts over the chest and buttoned on the left. I took it off its hanger and tried it on. The jacket was rather too large for me all over, but I could wear it if I tied its belt. I kept it. I wore it even when I went to sleep, in case anyone tried to steal it from me.

Once we knew for sure that the owner of the house had escaped from the pocket we were in, we broke open the two locked cellars by the simple expedient of having the dispatch riders fling themselves bodily against the doors until they fell out of the walls, frames and all.

The first cellar was for food. Two whole hams hung from the ceiling, along with salami sausages and sides of bacon. There were several containers of cooking fat stacked on top of each other in one corner, and in another corner we found a sack of sugar. There was tinned meat and tinned milk, and a great many preserves.

We celebrated our break-in with a huge festive meal, and then shared out what was left. The cooking fat kept the kitchen going for eight days.

The second cellar was larger than the first.

'He knew what to hoard, and no mistake!' said one of the dispatch riders.

The second cellar contained radio valves, nothing but radio valves, thousands of them in their cardboard boxes, stacked right up to the ceiling in neat rows.

'We can use the radio again!' said the intelligence people, delighted. They collected all available radio sets and fitted new valves. That evening there were radios playing in all the men's quarters. We listened to music as we ate salami or ham. However, the new valves, like the old ones, would last only two or three hours before they burned out. We had no mains current, and were running all the radios off car batteries; the valves had not been designed for such a load.

As soon as one valve burnt out, we removed it and fitted another. We had plenty!

The C.O. sent for the Russian woman from the kitchen. She came and stood in front of him, smiling at us. 'You want me?' she asked, leaning over his table.

The C.O., looking rather awkward, adjusted his glasses and went rather pink. After a minute or so he said, 'We have to send you away.'

'No!' The Russian woman did not understand. 'Why?'

The C.O. picked up a paper from the table. 'It's an order. All Russian ancillary staff to be sent to an assembly camp.'

'And then?' she asked.

'Well, from there you'll be taken to Germany by ship,' the C.O. said.

'Not true!' cried the Russian woman. 'You have no ships! Not even ships to take your own German women back to Germany!'

'Yes, yes, we have!' The C.O. was trying to calm her down. 'If that's what the order says, then that's what it means!'

'You lie to me!' said the Russian woman.

'No, really!' said the C.O., not too sure of himself.

The Russian woman began to plead. 'Don't send me away!'

'It's an order,' the C.O. repeated.

The Russian woman grasped my sleeve. 'Lieutenant, sir, you help me!' she begged. 'Hide me! I don't want to go to camp. I want to stay here with you.'

'Look, it's no good, we can't possibly hide you. We must obey! You must obey too,' said the C.O. firmly.

The Russian woman fell to her knees, hands clasped. 'I will obey, always! I'll do anything! Please, please don't send me away!'

'Oh, for heaven's sake!' shouted the C.O., getting up and striding out of the room.

Next morning we took the Russian woman and her bundle of belongings to the assembly camp. She was crying as we handed her over.

'I wouldn't care to be a Russian girl these days,' the C.O. said to me as we left.

The smaller our pocket became, the more the paymaster drank. He took to lying among his stores, dead drunk, with increasing frequency, and did no real work at all.

'You can see his point,' said the C.O. 'After all, we're in the process of losing his country for him.' However, so as to give the paymaster something to do and at the same time get him out of the men's sight, he gave him a job down on the shore. There, the paymaster was to make preparations for our retreat by building big, strong rafts, so that we and the rest of the unit could cross the water and go on fighting on the other side. The C.O. gave him four soldiers to help with the work.

Before the paymaster left, he carried out the official in-structions to be followed in such circumstances by solemnly burning the contents of his cash box – an old cartridge box containing about a hundred and twenty thousand marks. Then, all in due form, he handed over his stores, though he kept back enough to give us several bottles of genuine French cognac as parting presents. He loaded the rest of his stuff into our last remaining motor vehicle, a small car, and drove off with his four men.

'Well, that gets *him* out from under our feet,' said the C.O., with a sigh of relief. 'And we're doing something about future contingencies too!'

Only two days later the paymaster sent us back a message that the work was making good progress, and he had taken the car to bits so that its parts could be built into the rafts.

We picked out a sergeant who had won the Knight's Cross and promoted him to the staff. Since no one else knew the first thing about it, he was given the paymaster's job.

We were sitting round a table in the little labourer's cottage, drinking our last remaining bottle. We lowered our heads every time we felt an impact. The firing was so close now that the whole cottage shook, and plaster was crumbling off the ceiling.

'They'll be here in an hour,' said the C.O., quite quietly. And then, in sudden agitation, he cried, 'But I don't want to be taken prisoner!' He went back to brooding over his mug of brandy.

As machine-gun fire began ripping into the thatched roof, I got up from the table, and went and crouched in a corner of the room, on the floor.

The C.O. stayed put, but he suddenly burst out, 'You must go to the General! At once! Quick, before it's too late! He must authorize our withdrawal!'

I buckled on my dispatch case and left the cottage, picking

a dispatch rider from among the men sheltering in the stable to take with me.

Our divisional command post was in the town, but no one knew exactly where the fighting was going on. There were no radio or telephone communications left, but we knew that we would have to cross the railway embankment in any case. There were three tracks at the point where we wanted to cross. Keeping well down in the undergrowth, we waited until there was a pause in the machine-gun fire raking the embankment.

Then I jumped up and ran for it. A gun was fired somewhere. I crashed head first into the undergrowth on the other side of the tracks, lost my steel helmet, found it and put it on again. My head hurt, but otherwise I was all right.

Somewhere in the midst of this inferno someone was playing a piano, loud and clear.

The dispatch rider too got safely across the tracks. In the ditch on the other side of the embankment we met a sapper, who showed us the way to the command post. Then we found we had to cross a street under enemy observation. There was the corpse of an officer lying by the cellar steps which led down to the General, on the far side of the street. The body was bloated and thickly covered with dust. Keeping my nose to the ground, I made my slow way across the filthy street, round the dead man, and down the top steps. It took me nearly a quarter of an hour.

The General was alone when I came in, sitting with his head in his hands. 'Well, what is it, young man?' he asked.

I delivered the C.O.'s request.

'Yes, yes, get out of there!' he replied, with a dismissive gesture. 'The further the better!'

We set off as fast as we could, leaving all our heavy equipment behind. We did not have very far to go. In half an hour's time we had all reached the spot where our rafts were beached.

The paymaster, so drunk that he was swaying on his feet, reported that all preparations for the crossing were completed. Under cover of dark, and using no lights, we assigned crews to the rafts, picked the rowers and the relief rowers, and then loaded the packs on the rafts.

The first crew got on board.

When the raft was fully loaded, the water did not even reach the top of the thick planks of which it was made. None the less, it seemed to be stuck. The crews of the other rafts pushed it off with their poles and oars.

The raft slid clumsily over the sand, rocked, and suddenly sank. The crew were up to their thighs in water.

We saved what we could of the packs, but the raft itself did not come up. It was floating out in open water, still submerged below the surface.

We tried the other rafts. They were all the same. They were too heavy, and would not even carry two men at once.

'Didn't you test them out?' asked the C.O.

'No,' admitted the paymaster, scratching his head.

We sat there on the bank, helpless. At the thought of being taken prisoner, some of the men lost their nerve and threw themselves into the icy water fully clothed, hoping to swim to safety. We got them back to land, with some difficulty. We were also having to protect the paymaster from the wrath of the disappointed soldiers.

Suddenly, someone said, 'Looks like a ferry over there!' We all ran pell-mell the way he had pointed.

As I ran, there was a burst of firing; the impact flung me to the ground. My leather jacket kept the worst off, but I bruised both knees, and blood came trickling through the holes I had made in my trousers. My legs hurt, but I dashed on.

Sure enough, there *was* a ferry. Thousands of men were waiting at the landing-stage to be taken across the water, everyone pushing to go first. The landing-stage itself was under heavy fire, with bombers circling overhead. We crouched in the ditches, praying to reach safety, and towards morning we had all crossed on the ferry and landed on the opposite bank.

We marched all day.

The road was a corduroy track in the sand, between rows of pine trees. Sand got into our boots, stuck to our wet uniforms, blew into our eyes, mouths and noses. Exhausted, we dragged ourselves on. Hardly any of us had saved a pack, and no one had anything to eat. We quenched our thirst from pools of water.

There was only one house on the whole stretch of road, and that had been turned into a hospital; the staff there sent us on.

We did come to a few houses in the afternoon, and our C.O. begged for soup or bread, but an officer told us we could not stay there either, and we got nothing. Our legs were giving out. We had to stop more and more often for rests. Then at last, towards evening, we reached a village. The soldiers found a barn and some stables which were not yet crammed to overflowing, and they simply crawled in with the other people already there and fell asleep.

No rations were issued.

Seven officers, myself among them, found a bit of space in a room inside the farmhouse. There were fifteen refugees already there, men, women and children, either waiting for ships to take them away or hoping that we would counter-attack and win them back their houses and farms.

We pushed our way in among the refugees just as we were, wet and dirty, and fell asleep on the floor at once.

Next morning, the people shared what little bread they still had with us, and as I huddled on the floor, wrapped in a blanket and gnawing a dry crust, a woman darned the knees of my breeches with grey wool.

Ten men shared a loaf, and everyone got fifty grams of horsemeat sausage a day. The kitchen staff had nothing they could cook.

'I'm going to get hold of a cow!' said the C.O. 'You come with me!'

There was an administrative officer from the service corps sitting at the entrance to the cowshed, in the place partitioned off for milking. He let us pass without comment. There were over a hundred cows in the cowshed, black and white cows with thin flanks. Their racks were empty, and they kept lowing with hunger.

The C.O. turned to the service corps man. 'Why aren't you feeding these animals?'

'No cattle feed,' he said.

'Let them out, then, so they can graze!'

'We haven't enough men to guard them,' replied the service corps man.

'Why do you need to guard them when they're grazing?' asked the C.O.

The service corps officer laughed. 'If we didn't they'd get slaughtered.'

Baffled, the C.O. stared at him. 'And why not?'

'They belong to the local inhabitants!'

'But the local inhabitants have left!'

'Well, when they come back they'll need their cattle so as to get their farms going again,' said the service corps officer.

'Oh, come, do you really believe that?' asked the C.O. 'Do

you honestly think those people will ever be back? Why, in eight days' time we'll be gone ourselves!'

The other man shrugged his shoulders. 'Not for me to decide.'

'We are hungry, and so are the cattle.' The C.O. made a last effort to convince him. 'Let those cows out before they die, and then at least the men will get something to eat! I'm taking a cow now. I'll be responsible!'

'Sorry!' said the service corps officer, smiling slightly. 'I've got my orders.' He took out his pistol and laid it on the table in front of him. 'And I'll enforce them with this if necessary.'

The sergeant who had taken over the paymaster's job shrugged his shoulders. 'I've collected a good bit of stuff again,' he said. 'I'll be needing a lorry for all our bits and pieces when we move off.' He smiled. 'And I suppose we will be leaving here, quite soon!'

'Have you tried the service corps?'

He dismissed that idea. 'They're short of equipment themselves. Mind you,' he added, 'there are plenty of vehicles about – you only have to open any shed door and you'll find something, a pretty little trap or a heavy great farm cart. Only there aren't any horses to pull 'em, that's the trouble.'

'Yes, well, we all switched over to horse-drawn vehicles when the motor fuel gave out, and by now we've eaten most of the horses.'

'Well, what am I going to do?' the sergeant asked. 'I was so pleased to have got a few stores together after we were nearly starving – I can't just leave them here! And I can hardly ask the men to pull a cart for me.'

'How many horses would you need?'

'At least two,' said the sergeant.

'Give me till tomorrow,' I told him.

However, there was not much hope in his face as he turned and left the cellar.

'Can you by any chance lay hands on a couple of countrymen who know about horses?' I asked one of our dispatch riders.

'Well, sir, we did take on two old fellows from the Volkssturm organization a few days ago,' replied the dispatch rider. 'They used to work on a farm somewhere around these parts.'

'Send them to me.'

A quarter of an hour later the two old men came into the cellar. Their backs were bent, and they looked as if they were used to hard work on the land.

'Do you know anything about horses?'

They both nodded.

'Well, we've got fifteen hours. I want you to go and sleep now till it's dark. Then we'll wake you. You're to get two horses from somewhere – it doesn't matter where. Take them from a stable or a field, but watch out for sentries; you don't want to get shot at. And don't on any account get caught. Two horses – two good draught-horses, that's what we need, understand?'

'Yes, sir,' said the two old men.

We were quartered in a large house with a toolshed and a small pigsty. Day and night, fugitives passed along the road. Some of them had carts of some sort, but most had nothing but their bundles. They were all making for the port, hoping to get out of this pocket. As soon as darkness fell they would invade the house along with their children and their bags and baggage. They did not ask anyone's permission, just lay down and slept anywhere they could find room: on the stairs, in the attic, the cellars, the shed, the pigsty.

Very late one evening a young and pregnant woman came asking for shelter. She looked worn out, and held on to the door frame to support herself as she spoke. The stairs were already crammed and all the rooms filled to overflowing; the only spare place to sleep was in my room.

Eventually the great trek came to a halt. The fugitives were camping in their thousands on the quays and streets of the harbour town; there were not enough ships to get them out.

And the young woman stayed. She tidied my room, tended the stove, cleaned my things and made my sandwiches for me. I soon got quite used to her, and when I came back to my room it seemed far more homelike than before. She would often disappear for long periods during the day, and I found that I missed her.

Occasionally she went to help in a field dispensary, and in the evening she would bring back alcohol and concoct drinks from it.

Suddenly, news came that ships had arrived, and the flow of refugees started moving again. Next morning I helped her settle her rucksack on her back and said I would accompany her down to the road.

At first she demurred; then, suddenly, she turned and ran to the pigsty. After a while she came back with two old people and introduced them. 'My parents.'

Before I could say anything, the old man explained, his voice harsh and hostile. 'I told her not to mention us! If you'd known *we* were here my daughter would never have been allowed to stay with you so long, sir. And she was better off in your bed than in the pigsty or the road.'

When our own quarters came under fire we moved into the foxholes we had dug in readiness. A particularly large one had been dug for the C.O., and I went in with him. Down in the foxhole there was really only room for the two of us to sit face to face without moving. The moment we leaned either forward or back we bumped into the damp mud walls and got filthy. We had to stand up to change sides, though we could not stand right up, because the hole was too shallow.

The dispatch riders crawled down the entrance to our foxhole on hands and knees, put their heads in, received orders, still in this position, and made their way out backwards into the open again.

We huddled close together, and even put our arms round each other, but still we froze at night and could get no sleep.

When the firing outside slackened off a bit, the C.O. went out. 'My feet were about to freeze off!' he said on his return.

Next morning we dashed over to a house, under fire. We could not find what we were after, so during a pause in the firing we went on. In the fourth house we struck lucky. We made our way back to our foxhole on our stomachs, laden with sheets and feather-beds.

I moved over to the dispatch riders' foxhole for an hour, while one of them helped the C.O. fix up our own place. They hung white sheets over the sides and padded the bottom with feather-beds; they even fastened one feather-bed just under the plank roof.

'What's that supposed to do – smother a direct hit?' I asked.

'No, no,' said the C.O., perfectly seriously. 'It's to stop us hitting our heads so hard in the daytime, and at night we'll take it down and sleep under it.'

The dispatch riders used the rest of the bedclothes to fit up their own foxhole.

Two days later it rained, and water ran into our hole from on top, from below and from all sides. We had to huddle there among filthy, brown sheets, on our wet and soggy feather-beds, shivering with cold, until we moved on.

The sergeant was the first to spot the barrel.

It was lying on the edge of the trench, which was only chest-high. 'We've got to get there!' he said.

We crawled along the narrow trench on hands and knees; we did not meet anyone. The whole area was under constant fire. The heaviest of the firing was directed at the woods, but if you lifted your head only slightly above the top of the trench there would be a hail of artillery fire coming at you.

The sergeant sniffed. 'Beer!' he called back to me, going faster.

We trampled through some beery mud, and then we were within reach of the barrel. It had a hole shot in the bottom of it, and a thin stream of beer was splashing on to the edge of the trench and trickling away into the earth.

The sergeant put his finger in the stream of beer and licked it. 'Not even too warm!' he said happily.

However, we had no flasks or mugs with us.

'No good using our helmets,' said the sergeant. 'They'd stick to our heads afterwards. We'll have to hurry, though, or it will all run away!' He crept round the next corner of the trench and came back almost at once with a small, dirty, battered tin pail.

I shook my head, but he nodded. Carefully, he put the pail under the stream of beer, took a piece of newspaper from his back trouser pocket, cleaned the pail out with the newspaper and the first of the beer he had caught in it, and then refilled it and offered it to me.

I took it, and drank.

There was a wounded man on the edge of the wood; a shell splinter had torn away his lower jaw, and he kept moving his tongue about, helplessly gurgling something incomprehensible.

Further on!

We ran past him, into the wood. There were dead and wounded everywhere. A man hit in the stomach screamed when he saw us, then shouted curses after us. An elderly captain was crying quietly and calling for his mother. One man was trying to crawl, leaving a trail of blood behind him the same width as his shoulders.

On!

More firing. We ran. We looked for cover. There wasn't any.

Heavy fire screeched over us, shells burst in the treetops above our heads. Splinters were flying everywhere. Bits of branch toppled to the ground, leaves came fluttering down after them. A tree swayed, creaking.

On!

Split and naked tree trunks, their tops blown away, pointed skyward. Four or five dead men were huddled together by the side of the path, as if trying to shelter.

On – further on!

We ran on, panting. There was more firing . . .

Fear . . .

The sergeant found a hole; I went in after him. A narrow hole . . .

Damn that sergeant . . . *he'd* be all right . . . I was going to get hit by the shell splinters . . .

Appalling fear rising in me . . .

My knees drove into his back.

Down . . . down . . .

Screams . . .

Crazy fear . . .

An explosion!

It was over!

Any wounds?

Out of here, then, fast!

Far too slowly, the sergeant stood up. He had been kneeling on top of a dead man.

On . . .

Back Again

The Chief of Staff was busy, and I was told to wait in a neighbouring bunker till he could attend to me. The roof of this bunker consisted of at least four really good thick planks, and before you got into the bunker proper you went down through a solidly built passageway. Inside, the walls were even roughly plastered, and there were real beds, and lockers, and electric light.

Two officers were sitting at a table, one with his back to the entrance, the other hidden from me by the first. They were so absorbed in their card game that they had no time to notice me. I sat down in an armchair near the door and waited, passing the time by watching the two players.

They had just finished a game, and the winner was pointing out the loser's mistakes to him, while the loser justified his method of play to the winner. The argument was getting quite heated when the loser produced a bottle from under the table and filled both their glasses. They tossed back the contents, then shuffled the cards and began another game. I noticed that the officer with his back to me wore no shoulder-straps.

Suddenly the bunker door opened and a private came in, giving a rather casual salute. Without bothering to stand to attention, he went over to the players, looked at the cards held by both of them, and said, searching in his trouser pocket with one hand, 'It's all ready. Cases stowed away and all.'

'I just want to win this game,' said the loser of the last one.

And so he did. Satisfied, he gathered up the cards and stuffed them into his breast pocket, took another large gulp from the bottle, and offered it to his opponent. When the other officer refused, he handed the half-empty bottle to the private. 'The rest's for you! Cheers!' Then he slapped both thighs and intoned, in an ecclesiastical manner, 'Very well, then – o–o–off we go!'

Both officers rose, stretched and came towards the door. Each of them wore a crucifix on his chest.

It was the first time in the whole war I had set eyes on an Army chaplain.

We left so suddenly that I had to leave behind everything I possessed. We were not marching now, we were running, running to the harbour.

The soldiers were groaning as they stumbled over the rough tracks, footsore, their boots full of sand. No one dared stop, even to shake the sand out of his boots. The great thing was not to miss the boat!

When we did reach the harbour we found crowds of people waiting on the quay: old men, women, children, soldiers, convicts, everyone. Some of the soldiers were weeping openly with fear and disappointment.

We spent the night in a school building, and posted sentries down by the quay. I spent the night going between the sentries and the school as we waited for the ships to come in.

The sentries had difficulty keeping awake. And still the ships did not come.

I did not lie down until dawn, and then I fell asleep at once. Through my dreams I half heard the others getting up, but I did not wake properly until I heard singing.

The school building was empty, and the sun was shining outside. The singers were our dispatch riders, standing there in front of me. When the song was over, one of them stepped forward. 'For you, sir! Because you lost everything.' He offered me a crumpled handkerchief.

The next man gave me half a cake of shaving soap, and the third part of a bar of chocolate.

They wished me many happy returns of the day. It was my twentieth birthday.

It was raining steadily. My cap, my leather jacket, my battledress blouse, my breeches, even the rags wrapped round my feet inside my boots were soaked.

And still it went on raining.

This was the second night we had spent standing on deck in the rain, in the middle of the forecastle, shoulder to shoulder, one man's back pressed against another man's chest. We were six officers and seventy men, the remains of our division.

And still it went on raining.

Old men, women and children were crowded on deck, standing cheek by jowl right up to the railing. They were perched on the ship's superstructure, on the steps, right up to the command bridge.

And still it went on raining.

Down in the hold wounded men, and women in labour, the dead and the newborn, lay side by side, the rain beating in on their faces through the open hatches.

And still it went on raining.

Our ship was in fact a freighter, on her maiden voyage, sent out from the shipyard for this purpose before she was properly finished. There were no boats, and no life-jackets. Nor was there room to accommodate so many people.

And still it went on raining.

We leaned against each other, exhausted, hemmed in by

the refugees all around us. Most had eaten nothing for days. Some people fainted, and hung there among the others, their knees bent.

And still it went on raining.

'This rain is just what we want,' someone beside me said. 'Good weather for keeping bombs and torpedoes off.'

And still it went on raining.

'What if we bump into a mine, though?' someone else asked.

I needed to go to the lavatory. Small wooden cubicles had been set up by the railing for this purpose, and I tried to get to one of them from where I was standing. But not even the men standing closest to me would give way to let me through.

I had to stay put.

And it rained.

I waited, and my need grew more urgent. I tried yet again . . .

No good.

No one would give up his place, or even change position, and anyone who was disturbed by a movement just cursed or kicked or hit out.

'Do it here,' said the man next to me, quietly.

I pretended not to have heard him. I shifted from one foot to the other, staring up at the sky, with the raindrops splashing into my eyes. I kneaded my hips and thighs with my fists. I held my breath . . .

'Oh, go on, sir, shit and get it over with, and then stand still!' snorted the man behind me.

Tears came into my eyes. I undid my belt and looked around me; I apologized to the company at large. Under cover of my jacket I unbuttoned my trousers.

No one was taking any notice of me.

I slowly let my trousers down. I wanted to squat . . . but the others would not budge. Their eyes were closed, and they were muttering with annoyance because of the way I was moving about.

Half standing and surrounded by other people, I relieved myself. They did not even move the toes of their boots aside. I glanced around me, wondering.

'Don't you worry, sir!' said my neighbour cheerfully. 'The rain will wash it away!'

Peace

It was getting light, and the clouds broke. The rain stopped and the sun came out. And now our troubles began.

Suddenly four or five thousand people on deck began to scream at once, screaming in terror and despair . . .

A plane was coming over from the north, flying low above the water. First it was a tiny dot, then it grew, made for our ship, gained height – and turned away.

It was not until we sighted land that everyone finally calmed down.

Our ship came into Copenhagen harbour and berthed during the morning, under a cloudless sky. Slowly, the exhausted passengers went on shore.

We left the ship too. I staggered off; my legs hardly seemed to belong to me any more. I slipped, beside the wall of a hut, and found myself sitting on the wet pavement.

The C.O. sent me into the town to look for quarters. I staggered off across the quay.

There was what looked like an impenetrable wall of human beings on the far side of the barrier, men and women with bitter faces, all staring at me. Their eyes were hostile, their fists clenched.

Reluctantly, I went on, towards the crowd. My boots squelched with moisture at every step I took, and the darned knees of my breeches were black and stiff. My soaked leather jacket was still dripping, I had several days' growth of beard on my chin, and I was tired out . . .

Ten more steps before I reached those threatening faces.

I couldn't see any way out of this. Eight more steps, five more steps . . .

An old woman ran towards me, her hands stretched out, her fingers spread.

I ducked, raising my arm to protect my face . . .

She flung her arms round my neck and hugged me; she was crying. 'Peace!' she shouted, in broken German. 'It's peace!'

There never was a good war, or a bad peace.

(Benjamin Franklin, 1706–1790)